KT-525-672

LOVE'S SWEET SECRETS

When her parents die, Melanie comes home to run their guest house and to try to win the Jubilee Prize for her father's garden. But her sister, Angela, wants her to sell the property, and her boyfriend, Michael, wants a partnership and marriage. Just before the Spring opening, Paul Hunt arrives and helps Melanie when the garden is attacked by vandals. After the news is splashed over the national papers, guests cancel. Then real danger threatens. But who is the enemy?

Books by Bridget Thorn
in the Linford Romance Library:

ISLAND QUEST
HER STOLEN HEART

BRIDGET THORN

LOVE'S SWEET SECRETS

WORCESTERSHIRE COUNTY COUNCIL
CULTURAL SERVICES

Complete and Unabridged

LINFORD
Leicester

First published in Great Britain in 2005

First Linford Edition
published 2005

Copyright © 2005 by Bridget Thorn
All rights reserved

British Library CIP Data

Thorn, Bridget
    Love's sweet secrets.—Large print ed.—
Linford romance library
1. Romantic suspense novels
2. Large type books
I. Title
823.9'14 [F]

ISBN 1–84617–032–X

Published by
F. A. Thorpe (Publishing)
Anstey, Leicestershire

Set by Words & Graphics Ltd.
Anstey, Leicestershire
Printed and bound in Great Britain by
T. J. International Ltd., Padstow, Cornwall

This book is printed on acid-free paper

1

'Dad would have loved to see the pergola finished. He won't see the Nymphenburg rose in bloom either.'

Melanie looked at her sister and nodded.

'That's why I have to keep the garden going, at least until the Silver Jubilee competition. He was so hoping to win that.'

Angela sighed, pushed back her hair, which was almost as dark as Melanie's, but much shorter, and then laughed.

'I know. It would be difficult to let it go now, but it means almost a year before we can sell the house. Remember I agreed before David lost his job, but now David and I need the cash. If he doesn't get another job before the redundancy money runs out I'll have to go out to work again, and I don't want to do that until the children are a bit older.'

'I've loaned you all I can,' Melanie reminded her, feeling slightly guilty.

Then she asked herself why Angela shouldn't work while David was unemployed and could easily look after the children. She herself worked very hard, and Angela could temp as a secretary.

'And you get your share of the profits from the guest house every month,' she added.

She turned and looked at the old house, the walls covered in creepers, the mullioned windows shining in the spring sunshine. She'd like to keep it, carry on with the business her parents had established, and keep the garden, too, in memory of her father, but she couldn't afford it.

Half of it belonged to her sister. Was it too sentimental to delay selling just so that her father's garden, his pride and joy, might stand a chance of the Jubilee prize? He wasn't around anymore to know if he won or not. Yet somehow she was sure he would be aware.

She grinned suddenly. Imagining her father sitting on a cloud somewhere in heaven and looking down at his garden was a fantasy.

Angela was looking back along the rose pergola, too.

'Hello, it seems as if one of your guests has arrived. Wow, there's a Mercedes! Why does a man who can afford a Mercedes stay at a small guest house instead of a posh hotel?'

'Our guest house is a very superior one! We charge hotel prices, so don't mock. I'd better go and do the welcoming-hostess bit. It's Jane's day off, and Susie isn't quite up to speed yet. She's more likely to be sitting on the reception desk drinking coffee and demanding to know how much his car cost than explaining the system.'

'I don't know why you employ her,' Angela grumbled as they walked back towards the house.

'She's a good worker, if she's told what to do. And we don't have all that much choice in a small village. Westford girls usually head for the bright lights as soon as they can, like I did.'

She could see the man getting out of the car now. He was tall, and his fair hair gleamed gold in the sunlight. It was long, brushing his collar, and reminded her of Michael Forster, who had also been blond and very conscious of his carefully windswept hairstyle.

'Dishy,' Angela murmured. 'I'll be off, Mel. See you in a few days.'

Melanie nodded and turned away from Angela. Michael was in the past and she did her best not to think about him. She thrust aside the memories and adopted her professional greeting smile.

'Good afternoon. Mr Hunt?'

'Hi. Yes, I'm Paul Hunt.'

'Melanie Hetherington. Welcome to Westford Court. I hope your stay with us will be a pleasant one. I'll show you your room if you'll come with me. I'll send someone for your bags later.'

'I haven't much. I can manage,' he

said, slinging a suit bag on to his shoulder and picking up a smaller sports bag.

Melanie smiled with real gratitude. The someone to assist him would have been her, since they had no porter. Susie's father helped out on Saturdays with some of the jobs, but he worked at a nearby garage during the week. She led the way up the wide, oak staircase, and along a corridor to the farthest room.

'Being a corner room it overlooks all the garden apart from the front,' she explained. 'Bathroom's through there, and if there's anything else you need please ask at Reception. Are you staying in for dinner?'

'If that's convenient. Eight o'clock, please.'

'The menu's here, and the wine list. If you wish you can phone your choice down beforehand.'

'Great. Are there many people here?'

'Just you and a couple with two teenage children tonight. We're full for the weekend, then for the rest of Easter week.'

'I suppose people come to see the gardens. The village is famous for them, and I'm hoping to see them all during the open week.'

Melanie looked at him, suddenly interested. He didn't seem the typical gardening enthusiast, too young, early thirties, she guessed. And his hands were long and slender, well shaped. She couldn't imagine him double digging or pulling up weeds. Most men, she'd discovered, developed their interest in gardening when they retired and mostly, even then, it was for the vegetable growing, not the shrubs and flowers Westford was noted for.

'Feel free to look at ours whenever you like. I'll leave you now, Mr Hunt. Let us know if there's anything else we can do to make your stay a pleasant one.'

As she went back down the stairs she glanced at her watch. It would be dark soon, but she had an hour before she had to start cooking. She found Susie in the small room they'd converted to a bar.

'Susie, listen for the phone, please. I hope Mr Hunt will phone down what he wants for dinner, and you'd better be ready to open the bar for him. I'll be in the greenhouse if you need me.'

'Sure, Mel. Dishy bloke, that. Is he married?'

'I didn't ask, and if you do, I'll scalp you!'

Susie laughed.

'Don't fuss! I'll leave him for you if you want him. Too old for me, even if he is gorgeous!'

She was irrepressible, Melanie thought, smiling. Some of the more dignified guests looked surprised, even disapproving, when they first encountered Susie, but so far, luckily, none of them had refused to come back. They depended on regular visitors, her father always having preferred not to advertise too widely.

'I want it to be thought of as a

second home,' he'd explained when Melanie, new to London and the aggressive marketing techniques of Michael, her new boss, had suggested adverts in the glossy magazines. 'Besides, if I had those costs I'd have to put up my prices. We do well enough.'

He'd been right, she thought as she went back down the pergola walk and through the archway in the hedge, to where the greenhouses were screened away. She set the timer. That was always necessary or she'd become so absorbed in pricking out her seeds, or tending the older plants, she'd forget the time. With dinner to cook for five guests, she didn't dare let that happen.

She'd pricked out a tray of begonias, and was covering them with sheets of glass when a shadow fell across the bench.

'Miss Hetherington, sorry if I startled you. This looks a very professional set-up,' she heard Paul Hunt say.

'My father planned it.'

'What are they?'

'Begonias. I use them in the beds on the driveway, and some of the containers. They are so colourful against the stone flags.'

'You're the gardener?'

'I trained as a florist, but when my father died I came home and took over the garden,' Melanie said briefly.

She didn't want to have to explain her motives to a stranger who might not understand.

'Tell me about the Silver Jubilee prize,' he said. 'Do you mind if I sit here while you work?'

'Of course not.'

Melanie picked up another tray of seedlings and began pricking out.

'Westford has been opening its village gardens for years, collecting for the local hospice. Twenty-five years ago they began to give prizes, one for each season, to the garden the visitors voted the best. Then there is the overall prize for the year.'

'How is that decided?'

'There's a complicated formula based

on how many people visited each garden and where it came in the seasonal competitions.'

'How often did your father win it?'

She was surprised.

'How did you know he won?'

'Guessed. His garden is superb. I know I haven't seen the others yet, but they'd have to be pretty special to beat this. And now you're keeping on the tradition?'

'Well, just for this year. Then we'll have to see.'

'This year is the Silver Jubilee, with a special prize, isn't it?'

She nodded.

'A glossy magazine is doing a big feature at the end of the year. We need to attract more visitors to the village as it costs more every year to fund the hospice.'

'I see. Well, good luck, Miss Hetherington. I need to make some phone calls, so I'll leave you to your work.'

He turned to go just as the timer pinged.

'What's that?'

'To remind me I'm needed else-where.'

She wasn't sure why she avoided telling him she'd be cooking his dinner. It didn't perhaps strike the right note if he knew they didn't have a chef.

Susie doubled as barmaid and waitress, and later on in the evening she reported that all the guests had gone to their rooms.

'So let me wash up. Those girls, and their parents, were knackered after riding all day. That's the trouble with townies. No moderation. They'll be too stiff to move tomorrow, and Mr Hunt said he'd work to do.'

'I'm off to bed myself soon. There's a lot to do tomorrow, ready for opening on Saturday.'

Melanie was up by six. She tied her hair in a ponytail to keep it out of the way, pulled on old jeans and a thick red sweatshirt. Downstairs, in the boot room by the kitchen, she thrust her feet into heavy boots and picked up a

11

wicker basket. She would deadhead the daffodils first, sweep the paths, then give the grass on the main lawns the first light cut, and all would be ready for opening the garden the following day. She'd have time in the afternoon to bake the cakes for the refreshments each house offered visitors. Thank goodness Jane was back to see to the other cooking.

The sun was rising above the fruit trees in the orchard at the end of the garden. It was always left as a wild flower meadow, and the trees were casting long shadows across the grass and the flowers. Melanie frowned. It looked different, but with the sun in her eyes it was difficult to see. Then as she walked nearer she gave a start of dismay.

Daffodil flowers lay all over the grass. The heads had been chopped off, she realised, as she came closer, with shears. The last of the snowdrops, which a month earlier had covered the ground, were drooping, as were the remaining crocus flowers. The blue-bells, just coming into flower, were shrivelled and the stems were brown.

'What on earth?' she exclaimed.

She dropped to her knees to look closer at the stricken plants, and saw the patches left where weed killer powder had not caught them. Who could have done this? Why? Was it to spoil her chance of winning an award? Was there anyone in Westford who could be so wicked?

2

'What's happened? Vandalism, do you think?' Melanie heard someone say and glanced up to see Paul Hunt looking at the ruined display.

She took a deep breath to steady her voice.

'Weed killer, I think, apart from the shears. It's a funny sort of vandalism! If I could catch the devils I'd drown them in weed killer and use the shears on tender parts of their anatomies!'

He was walking round, bending to examine some of the flowers.

'Not mindless. This was very deliberate. Who's your main rival for the prize?'

She was glad he'd seen the point. It saved time explaining how fanatical some gardeners could be, even though she couldn't believe it of her friends and neighbours.

'Dad nearly always won, especially the spring opening. The next best is Tom Harvey, at Ashcroft. But I can't believe Tom would do anything like this! We've always been good friends, swapping cuttings and seeds, and he's on the parish council.'

'Doesn't necessarily make him an upright citizen.'

'I'm sure Tom is. If her garden were better, I'd suspect Mrs Travers, at The Lodge. She's a spiteful hag at times, but it wouldn't help her. But what can I do? We open tomorrow.'

She was beginning to panic. She'd been horrified at the wanton destruction, but Paul Hunt's appearance had distracted her, and she hadn't been able to think ahead.

'Collect the daffodil heads,' he suggested. 'It'll look as though they've been dead-headed. Then do a high cut this afternoon when it's dried a bit, to take off the other flowers and most of the leaves. The lower parts aren't damaged so badly. They won't show.'

He captured the hands she was waving around and hauled her to her feet.

'But it's ruined the overall effect,' she said.

'You've daffodils and a few early tulips elsewhere. There's plenty of blossom, a whole hedge of forsythia still partly in bloom, and the magnolias are splendid. Only this part's been damaged. What's a few snowdrops and bluebells? Give me that basket and I'll get on with collecting up the daffodils while you do whatever it was you were planning for today. By the way, dinner last night was superb. Please congratulate the chef.'

'You can't change your plans to help me,' she protested.

'I'm here for a break, and some fresh air will do me good. I spend too much time indoors.'

Melanie raised her eyebrows. He was lightly tanned, even so early in the year, but he may have been on a skiing holiday recently, or lazing on a beach somewhere exotic. He wore jeans and a loose jacket, under which was a forget-me-not blue sweatshirt, which matched the blue of his eyes. Mentally she shook herself. What was she doing wasting time contemplating the colour of a man's eyes, even if he was, as Susie had said, dishy?

'You're kind. And I'm grateful.'

'Go and check that everything else is OK. It looked it as I came through, but I didn't see everywhere. I might have missed something.'

Melanie left him to it while she went round the rest of the garden. To her relief, all was well, and she began to sweep the paths.

Paul Hunt found her an hour later.

'Right, that's the daffodils cleared. It all looks magnificent. I have some work to do after breakfast, but I'll do the lawns after lunch. Can I eat here or is there a pub which does meals?'

Melanie looked at him, horrified.

'Oh, no! You haven't had any breakfast yet! I'm so very sorry! I

17

should have thought. We don't serve it before eight unless people ask.'

'It's still only half past eight,' he said. 'Have you eaten?'

She shook her head.

'I don't always bother. I get up as early as I can, and I've been so busy out here the past few weeks, using up all the daylight, I forget.'

'Not good for you. Come on, there's no more you can do here until the grass dries a bit.'

Melanie left him to go and wash, while she went into the kitchen. Jane Dodd, Susie's mother and Melanie's dearest friend as well as her main employee, was loading the dishwasher.

'That Mr Hunt's not down yet,' she grumbled. 'The others are all finished and they'll be out all day, even though they're complaining all their muscles ache. It won't help if they do too much and strain themselves.'

'Mr Hunt will be down soon. He's been helping me in the garden.'

'Helping you?' Jane gave her a

searching look. 'My Susie was going on about him. Film star, she said he was like.'

'He's been kind. Someone's ruined the spring flowers in the orchard,' she explained, making coffee and toast while Jane, gasping in horror, assembled bacon and sausages and eggs near the cooker.

'Who could have done such a thing? It's not like Westford folk to be so nasty. I suppose it might have been that incomer, what's her name, at Friar's Mead. Stupid name to give a house built yesterday!'

'I think it's Mrs Seton-Woodward.'

'That's it. Double-barrelled and too snooty to give the time of day to anyone she meets in the shop.'

'But her garden's so new! She surely can't hope to win a prize.'

'My Jim said she had a big landscaping firm from London there for weeks. He met the chaps in the pub, and they said nothing was too good for her — statues, pergolas, ponds and a gazebo, whatever that is when it's at home.'

'I don't think that's quite the sort of garden visitors to Westford expect,' Melanie said, smiling.

'No, and Betty, my neighbour, said she ordered two dozen hanging baskets from the garden centre. She works there, you know.'

Melanie giggled.

'If she puts all of them up round her executive type neo-Georgian palace it'll look like a florist's shop! Seriously, Jane, who could it have been? If it's not somebody who's desperate for the prize, was it meant against me personally?'

'Oh, come on, Mel, who'd have it in for you? You haven't been back more than six months, and you were away in London for seven years before that.'

'You mean I haven't had time to make enemies? Then perhaps it's just kids after all. I've heard about them using paint-stripper on cars. They could have got hold of some weed killer and thought it was fun. The orchard's not overlooked, and they could have crossed the river easily enough. It's not deep, even at this time of year, and there's a couple of sandbanks only a hundred yards upstream.'

'Well, I'll keep my ears open, and tell Jim to do the same. That sounds like Mr Hunt. I'd better go and take his order.'

Melanie spent the rest of the morning tidying up, but she went to look at the river and the sandbanks, low miniature islands which forced it into three channels just past where her garden ended. A hedge separated it from the pasture next door, but it was possible to squeeze round the end of it without falling in the river. Perhaps she ought to extend it with a fence panel, right into the water.

The river was higher than she'd thought, and the sand was covered with a thin film of water. No footsteps remained. The field on the far side was a paddock containing a couple of ponies, bordered by a narrow lane with no houses. It would be possible to come this way unseen.

She was back in the greenhouse again when Paul Hunt appeared.

'Hi, there. I'm going to the pub for lunch. Will you join me?'

Melanie allowed her surprise to show.

'But — it's not necessary.'

'I'd like it, and you can explain the village to me, point out any of the local gardeners. I want to look at all the gardens when they open tomorrow, judge who might think they can rival you.'

'I don't think any of the really keen gardeners will be in the Three Crowns today,' she replied, grinning. 'They'll be looking for last-minute weeds, as I should be.'

'You have to eat, and you can look for intruders of the vegetable kind this afternoon, and I have to eat out. Your maid, Jane, told me.'

'She shouldn't have,' Melanie exclaimed. 'We provide meals if they're

22

wanted! Surely Jane wasn't rude to you?'

He laughed.

'Oh, she was perfectly polite, indeed pressed me to stay in, said what a treat it would be for her to stop all her other work to prepare me something, and indicated it would suit her fine if I were to take you off her hands, too.'

Melanie bit her lip. She would find out from Jane. He must be teasing, and his smile was devastating. Suddenly lunch at the Three Crowns sounded an excellent idea.

'You said you were a florist before,' he said half an hour later when they were sitting over lunch near a window in the Three Crowns. 'Where, in London or Oxford?'

'London. The firm supplied several large hotels and clubs in the West End as well as offices.'

'Oh, you mean those plastic palm arrangements in wooden boxes?'

'No, I do not! We used real plants,' Melanie said indignantly before she saw he was teasing her. 'And the usual wedding bouquets, wreaths and flowers by Interflora from husbands who'd forgotten their wives' birthdays.'

'Susie told me you were a partner, but sold out to come back home.'

'Susie chatters too much about what doesn't concern her, and she doesn't know everything! I wasn't a partner, though I might have been in time. Still might be, I suppose. Michael, my boss, wanted to expand but he needs capital. I'm not sure he'll wait a year until I can sell this house, or if I'd want to go back,' she added almost to herself. 'There comes a time when one has to go forward, not back.'

She glanced up at him as she spoke, and surprised an unexpectedly bleak look in his eyes. Then he smiled and it was gone.

'Right then, to business. Are any of your rivals here?'

'Almost everyone here apart from the three men in business suits over in the far corner.'

'Everyone?'

She laughed at the surprise in his voice.

'You don't realise what the garden openings mean to Westford. It's almost a point of honour that people open up their gardens, all except the very old and infirm, or those with kids who need the space for football-mad children.'

'But not the main rivals, Tom, Mrs Travers and Mrs double-barrel?'

'Jane has been indiscreet!'

'Don't blame her. It was Susie, as a matter of fact. She'd just heard when she brought me some coffee, and most indignant she was. Your staff are very loyal.'

'Jane came here when Mum and Dad opened it as a guest house. Dad could never have coped without them when Mum died. Susie had just left school then, so she came to work for him.'

'If you sell, they'll have to find other jobs.'

Melanie nodded.

'I know, and that's another problem.

There isn't much else for them here in the village. But Angela, my sister, needs her share of the cash and I can't afford to buy her out and keep it on. She only agreed we needn't sell until the end of the year because of the roses.'

'You could get a mortgage or a bank loan. It's a flourishing concern. Or a partner, perhaps.'

Melanie wondered suddenly what it was about him that made her confide such private concerns like this. He was a stranger, a paying guest, and she knew nothing about him.

'Well, I've time to decide. Look, Mr Hunt, it was — '

'Paul, please,' he interrupted.

She paused. He had a way of stopping her short whenever she tried to be more formal.

'Melanie then. There is really no need for you to help me this afternoon. I'll have time to mow all the grass myself.'

'I'd like to help. Incidentally, the names of the roses start with the initials of your names. Masquerade, Ena Harkness, Lolita. Your middle name is Jessica. What's the last rose like? I've not seen a Nymphenburg before. And it's the first Osiria I've seen in bloom. A beautiful rose, with that silver and deep blood red combination.'

Melanie was smiling.

'You worked it out? Well, Dad started the rose pergola when Angela was born. He insisted our names had to have twenty-five letters in them, and he planted a rose each birthday, to correspond with a letter. The Nymphenburg's a pinky orange with a lovely scent.'

'What would he have done if he'd had more children?'

'Started another pergola, of course!'

'And why stop at twenty-five? You could have had really long names and lots more roses. Did he expect you both to be married by then?'

She laughed.

'Probably. Angela was.'

He was amazingly easy to talk to, she

reflected as they walked back. She hadn't revealed so much to anyone before. Yet he'd revealed nothing about himself, what he did, why he was here, if he was married.

Stop it, she scolded herself. She was as bad as Susie, who wanted to know the marital status of every male over the age of sixteen and had no reservations about asking. The sneaking thought crept into her mind that she would no doubt discover this soon from Susie, and she could find out where he lived from the register, or back in the files from when he'd booked.

'I'll change and see you in the garden,' he said as they went in through the front door.

Susie was arranging flowers in a small vase on the reception desk, and winked at Melanie as Paul bounded up the stairs.

'I'd stick to him,' she said in a stage whisper. 'Mr Lennox rang.'

'Did he leave a message?'

Melanie's heart seemed to be beating

rather fast. It was over a month since Michael had rung. They'd exchanged desultory e-mails but hadn't spoken for weeks.

'No, said he'd get in touch later.'

'Thanks, Susie. Are all the rooms ready? We'll be full tonight.'

'Sure, and Dad's coming up after work. He said he's going to mount guard tonight with the dog to frighten them off. Can't have any more damage.'

Melanie went to put on her gardening clothes, marvelling at the kindness and loyalty of Susie's family.

'I'll get the mower,' Paul said as they walked into the garden a few minutes later. 'Where do you keep it?'

'The tool shed's beyond the greenhouses. I'll show you.'

'I suggest you get a stronger lock for here,' he said as Melanie opened the padlock which secured the door. 'That would be no deterrent, and they might try real damage next time.'

'I hope there won't be another time!'

'Why not, if it's really a rival for the prize?'

'I suppose you're right. But Jim Dodd, Susie's Dad, says he means to patrol tonight. He was in the army until he married Jane, and I suspect he'll feel it's like the old days. Do you want the tractor mower or the other?'

'The tractor might leave tyre tracks. It's still quite wet down by the river bank.'

Melanie nodded. She'd been prepared for that, for the ordinary mower was hard work. Most people, especially men, she thought, who like mechanical toys, would have chosen the tractor.

'If you're sure.'

'Quite. Then I'll do the lawns. I imagine you were planning to do that.'

'Yes, but I can do them when you've finished.'

He checked the mower over briefly, then grinned at her.

'Go and find a stronger padlock. Then finish that pricking out I disturbed you at yesterday, and as the house is full tonight I imagine there's plenty for you to do in the kitchen, chef.'

'Yes, sir!'

She knew she was blushing. She had Susie to thank, no doubt, that he knew she sometimes did the cooking, too, when it was Jane's day off. Had he known earlier when he'd sent compliments to the chef?

Trying to concentrate on his bossiness instead of his many attractions, she went to find a stronger padlock, and eventually had to get out her bike and ride the two miles to the local garage to buy one. In London, she'd had the use of one of the firm's vans, and hadn't yet bought a car of her own. She must look for a good, cheap one.

Jim wasn't at the garage when she got there. He worked in the maintenance department servicing farm machinery as well as cars, but Andrew, his boss, served her.

'Hear you had a spot of bother last night at the Court.'

She nodded. Did the whole village know? Several people in the pub had commiserated with her.

'I'm making the tool shed more secure,' she replied, handing him the biggest padlock he had on show.

'Let's hope it was just kids fooling about. Not nice to think any of the other villagers would do such a thing deliberately. Would you like me to come and fix something even stronger, or an alarm?'

'Jim's going to patrol, but later, perhaps, Andrew. I should have thought of it before. And perhaps an electric fence along the riverbank. That's where they got in, I'm sure. How much is this?'

She left him grumbling to himself about not knowing what the country was coming to when people had to barricade themselves into their own houses, and daren't leave a door open any more.

On the ride back to the Court, she went slowly, for the first time thinking seriously about if any of her rivals could have done such a thing. This year was more important than most, true, and the prospect of publicity in a glossy magazine would tempt some.

If she won, it would be good for her business. Were there any other businesses who would benefit by extra visitors? The Three Crowns? Andrew himself? The shop? The tearooms? Any of the artists and craftsmen who had come to live here and sold pottery and jewellery and paintings? Several pages of free publicity would benefit all of them.

Melanie sighed. The list of potential suspects was getting bigger by the minute, but she would not believe any of them could be so deceitful and mean. Westford wasn't like that. Yes, there was rivalry over the best gardens, but it was a friendly rivalry. She simply wouldn't believe anything else.

3

Saturday dawned warm, with clear skies, a perfect early spring day. Melanie was up by six to check the garden, but no more damage had been done. Jim Dodd went inside for a well-earned, substantial breakfast, but swore that after a few hours in bed he'd be back to watch over the garden during the afternoon.

'You've got to go and see the others, Melanie, see what the competition is,' he insisted.

Restless, Melanie began to set out the cups and saucers they'd need for the visitors. Many of the householders who had the space and the inclination provided coffee, tea and cakes, and it all increased the amount they could give to the hospice. Westford Court used the large conservatory attached to the side of the house, where some of the more exotic plants grew.

Paul Hunt had breakfasted early, and then gone out, Susie reported.

'And I don't think he's married,' she added, grinning. 'No wife would put up with granddad pyjamas, with a couple of buttons missing!'

'Susie!'

'I didn't pry, Mel, honest! They were strewn across the bed when I went to do his room, and I just folded them up. Of course, the buttons may have been torn off in the throes of passion,' she added, dropping her voice into a deep, husky tone.

'What kind of films do you watch?' Melanie asked, but couldn't help grinning.

Susie laughed. 'He said he'd be back after lunch.'

Ten minutes later Angela arrived, storming into the kitchen where Melanie was helping Jane with the washing up.

'Mel, what's this I hear about the trees in the orchard being cut down?'

'Just a few daffodil heads, Angela, no trees. How on earth did that rumour get around? As far as Westbridge, too. Sit down and have some coffee. It's still hot.'

Angela flopped into a chair.

'Well, that was what I was told. Mel, if the rivalry over the gardens is this bad, is it worth hanging on? You have no chance of the prize now.'

'It doesn't look so terrible, unless you know what was there. We've tidied it up.'

'We? Surely Jane and Susie have been too busy.'

Melanie hesitated. She knew her sister's tendency to jump to conclusions without a shred of evidence.

'It was Paul — Mr Hunt — the man we saw arriving when you were here before.'

'Paul, is it? That was fast work. I'd never have thought it of you. It took you years before you'd go out with Michael.'

'He was my boss, and the other girls

were jealous when he started to pay attention to me.'

'Is he coming down this week?'

'I have no idea. I doubt it. He hasn't been exactly persistent since I gave up my job.'

'He's kept in touch, hasn't he?'

'The odd e-mail.'

'Susie said he phoned.'

Melanie was becoming irritated.

'Susie says a good deal too much! Leave it, Angela. Have you come to help with the teas? You'd be very welcome. We always seem to get lots of customers. They seem to think I have a huge staff, being a guest house.'

Angela shrugged.

'I'll have to go back home after lunch, but I'll help until then.'

Soon the first visitors arrived, and Melanie was kept busy answering questions and selling the small pots of herbs she'd prepared. To her relief no-one remarked on the rather bare state of the orchard, minus the wild flowers, but they were all full of praise for the rest of the garden, and she began to hope that she might stand a chance of the prize after all.

She was snatching a sandwich in the kitchen, listening to Angela's complaints about the cost of all the dancing, swimming and music classes her children just had to attend, when Paul popped his head round the door.

'Jim says he's taken over from you, so may I come round the other gardens with you as soon as you're ready?'

'You don't have to,' Melanie protested. 'You have your own work to do.'

'Mr Hunt, Mel's told me how kind you've been to her. I'm Angela Constantine, Mel's sister. You're down here for work, are you?'

'No, just a break,' he replied. 'So I can easily spare the time to tour the gardens. Ten minutes, Melanie?'

'Yes, thanks. If you insist.'

'I wonder what he does?' Angela mused after he'd left. 'Be careful, Mel. A man that good looking's bound to be married. You don't want to get involved with a married man. I'm surprised he's down here alone.'

'Angela, stop it! I'm not getting involved with anyone. I must go and get ready.'

She escaped, her face burning, hearing Angela's laughter floating after her. When she came downstairs again, wearing clean jeans and a thin shirt, carrying a light jacket, Angela had gone, and she breathed a sigh of relief. She didn't think she'd be able to behave naturally with Paul if Angela were watching them.

Her sister had been scornful when she'd given up her job with Michael, convinced that he wanted marriage as well as a business partnership. She'd warned Melanie regularly that no man would wait for ever, and Melanie thought it was that as much as her need for the inheritance which caused Angela to press for a quick sale of the house.

Paul was waiting by Reception, chatting to a couple of new guests, but when he saw Melanie he smiled to them and came across to greet her.

'Lead on. You'll know the best route to follow to take in all your potential rivals.'

Melanie frowned. She'd almost forgotten.

'It must have been kids,' she said as they set off down the drive. 'I can't believe anyone would want to harm me in such a way.'

'Well, take precautions, anyway. Now, where first?'

Every one of the villagers they met seemed to have heard about the damage caused, and Melanie received lots of sympathetic remarks. She found herself eyeing these people, most of whom she'd known all her life and considered friends, wondering if one of them had been creeping secretly about her father's garden destroying his work.

Opinion seemed fairly evenly divided about the motive. Melanie was intrigued, when she had time to think about it, that it was the people who stood little chance of winning a prize who suspected sabotage, while those with the best gardens tended to believe it was random vandalism.

It was late when they returned to Westford Court. Paul had insisted on visiting as many gardens as they could, and chatting at length with the owners, who were all willing to display their plants and their knowledge.

'You need a break,' he said as they walked back up the drive. 'I'm taking you out for dinner. I hear there are some good restaurants in Westbridge.'

Melanie was about to protest, then she suddenly longed to get away from gardens and problems. She'd worked hard ever since her father had died six months before. He'd been ill for months before he died, and let the garden go a bit the last few months. She'd had to work hard to bring it back to its former perfection — and Paul was a most attractive man!

'Thanks, I'd like that. But I must have a shower first.'

'Me, too. It's hot work talking to gardeners.'

Melanie laughed. 'Including me?'

'Let's say I'd like to talk about something different with you this evening.'

She pondered what to wear. Would one of her smart London dresses be overdoing it? In the end she chose a cream silk dress, simple but superbly cut, and let down her hair, which floated round her shoulders in a dark cloud.

She was glad of her choice when Paul gave her an admiring glance, and when he drove her to the most expensive and exclusive restaurant in the area. Melanie knew tables had to be booked well in advance. How had he managed to get one at short notice? Had it been luck, a cancellation, or had he booked some time ago, intending to take someone else there?

She soon forgot her questions, for he was a most entertaining companion. He mentioned that he was a businessman, but didn't elaborate. He'd travelled extensively, from comments he made, but he didn't mention his home life.

He encouraged Melanie to talk about her London job, and it wasn't until they were drinking coffee in the comfortable lounge that either of them mentioned Westford.

'So who could it be?' he asked suddenly, and Melanie had to drag her mind back to her problems. 'I can see half a dozen gardens which might stand some chance of the prize, but of course they'll have to be as good in June and September.'

She nodded. 'Most of them are. The really keen gardeners would like us to open in winter, too, but the committee doesn't think it would be worth while. No-one wants to traipse round gardens when it's cold and wet and windy.'

'Who's on this committee? They do the organising, I gather.'

'Tom Harvey's the chairman, has been for years. Dad was the treasurer, but Mrs Travers has taken over.'

She added half a dozen other names, and Paul nodded.

'I remember, we saw all of those, but only a couple of them, apart from Tom and Mrs Travers, would stand a chance. Is there any benefit from being on the committee, towards getting a prize, I mean? Can they determine how the marks are awarded?'

Melanie shook her head slowly.

'The system's been the same for years. They fix the dates we open.'

'So they could choose ones that favour what they grow in their own gardens,' he interrupted.

'I suppose so, but it can't make so much difference. They do all the admin work, and collect the money to send to the hospice. I think it's our contribution that's enabled it to stay open the past few years.'

'Where is it? In the village? I haven't seen it.'

'It's a couple of miles out on the Westbridge road. It was a big manor house, but the family sold it in the

Fifties, I think. Death duties finished them and they couldn't keep it up. A charity converted it, but it's hard for them to pay their way.'

'Have any villagers been there, as patients, I mean?'

'Yes, several. It's a normal nursing home, too, so people don't have to be dying to find a place there. The hospice part is in a separate wing. Jane's mother went there when she was too frail to stay in her cottage. Tom's wife died of cancer and she was there the last few months. I believe Mrs Travers' sister was there, too, though she never lived in the village. All the old people want to be there if they can, it's so handy for relatives and friends to visit.'

She yawned suddenly, and apologised. Paul laughed.

'It's been a long day. Time we went,' he suggested.

Melanie almost fell asleep on the way back. The car was comfortable, and she was exhausted. Paul slipped a CD into the player and the music was soft and dreamy. She came to with a start when he drew up in front of the Court.

'Here we are.'

He was out of the car and opening her door before she'd gathered her wits together. As she climbed out he put his arm round her shoulders and gave her a quick squeeze.

'Come on, you're almost asleep.'

'I think I'll manage to climb up the stairs. Thank you for a lovely evening, and all your help.'

He walked with her to the front door.

'It's been my pleasure. Now you're not to worry. If it is someone trying to spoil things for you, we'll find out. Good-night, Melanie.'

He bent down and dropped a kiss on her cheek.

'Go in. I'll just have a look round to check, and find Jim.'

She smiled sleepily. She had such good friends, people like Jim, for instance, who gave up his sleep to guard what was, after all, just a garden.

As she reached the front door, she

realised it was standing open, light streaming out on to the steps and the drive. For a second she thought some other disaster had hit her, until she saw the man standing on the top step looking down at her.

'Michael! You startled me! You didn't say you were coming.'

'I thought you'd know I'd want to be with you when the gardens opened, Mel, but Susie tells me there isn't a room for me, that you're fully booked. You could have saved one for me. Am I expected to sleep in the car?'

He looked tired, and despite the moment of annoyance at his unreasonableness, Melanie felt sorry for him.

'If you'd asked I've have kept one for you. I'm sorry, but I need to take all the bookings I can get. Can't you stay with Daniel?'

'You know my brother only has a studio flat. I don't choose to sleep on his floor.'

Melanie frowned at his tone. Had he quarrelled with Daniel? His brother was an architect, and had recently moved back to Westbridge to join a firm there.

'I expect there's a room at the Three Crowns. If not there's a couple of hotels in Westbridge. Shall I phone them for you?'

He shook his head, and glared at Paul, who was standing a few yards away, looking at them.

'I'll take my chances, but if none of them can put me up I'll drive back to London. You clearly have other fish to fry down here in the sticks.'

Before Melanie could reply, he pushed past her and stalked across to the Range Rover parked under the trees. She hadn't noticed it in the shadows. He'd always scorned a van for himself, though his assistants had been forced to use one. It didn't match the image he wanted, he'd said, and carried just as many flowers if he ever had to go out himself to cover for one of the staff.

She watched as he clambered in, revved up sharply, and reversed out, then shot down the drive, spraying gravel over the lawns.

Why had he suddenly turned up? He'd implied, when she'd refused to sell the house and become a partner, that everything was over between them. Now he seemed to think differently. Had he come down to try and persuade her, or was he here for simple friendship and support this first time she'd been responsible for the garden?

4

Melanie was woken soon after midnight by frantic barking. She leaped out of bed and ran to the window of her bedroom, in the attics where servants had once slept. She flung the window fully open and leaned out. In the fitful light of the moon she could see shapes racing across the front lawn, and soon realised they were ponies, being chased by Jim's dog. She groaned. Their hooves would tear up the smooth grass, and if they trampled the borders they'd wreak havoc.

She dragged on jeans and a sweater over the T-shirt she slept in, and ran down to the kitchen. Her boots were there, and she thrust her bare feet into them, then ran outside. The barking had stopped now, and as she rounded the corner of the house she saw Jim holding the dog, trying to calm it.

'They came galloping down the drive, Mel,' he gasped. 'Did ye hear the shot?'

'Shot? No, just the dog barking. What shot?'

'Well, it sounded like a shot, near the gates. I reckon that was what scared the horses.'

'Well, we can look into that later. Tie up Blackie. He's making them more frightened, and we'll try to catch them.'

It took half an hour before the three ponies were rounded up. They had just rope halters, and were sweating with fear, snorting and with eyes rolling. Melanie tied them to the fence and Jim fetched some straw.

'We'd best give 'em a rub down. The night's cold,' he said.

'They're from the riding school, I think. I've seen this piebald around the village plenty of times. But how did they get out, and get here?'

'They've been turned out into the paddocks,' Jim said. 'Easy enough for someone to catch them and lead them here, then terrify them into stampeding. And Blackie was loose. He frightened them more before I could shut him up. I'm sorry, Mel. They've made a right mess of this grass.'

'It can't be helped,' Melanie said, working away at the piebald's coat. 'What about this shot you heard?'

'Well, at first I thought it was a poacher, out after rabbits. It startled me, being so close. But now I come to think clearly, it could have been a firework. There seemed to be several bangs, close together, like some of them make. It sounded loud in the night.'

'And enough to panic the ponies. It hasn't woken anyone else up,' she said, glancing up at the dark house. 'I didn't hear anything until Blackie began to bark.'

'No-one else would think much of that,' Jim said. 'They somehow expect dogs in the country. Shall we take them back now?' he asked a few minutes later.

Melanie shook her head.

'No, it's too dark to lead them along the lanes. We could get hit by a car, and we don't have lamps. I'll ring Felicity as soon as it's light and she can come and collect them. She won't miss them before morning.'

'It was just more vandalism,' Jim said gloomily. 'And a fat lot of good I did to stop it.'

'You couldn't have stopped it. You don't think they could have got out by themselves?'

'No. Felicity keeps those hedges tight, and she padlocks the gate.'

'Then how did anyone get them out?'

Jim shrugged.

'Easy enough, if you've the strength, to lift a gate off its hinges.'

'I'm going down there as soon as I've rung Felicity, to look for myself. Even if they did get out it doesn't explain why they came all the way here. I'd have expected them to stop and graze on the verges, or the green. It must be someone wanting to harm me, spoil the garden. But who?'

The question was unanswerable, and Melanie persuaded Jim to come in and have a cup of tea. She then went back to bed, lying down in her clothes in case there was a further alarm, but all was quiet. She lay sleepless, pondering again who might be so jealous or such a rival they had to cause her this damage and grief.

She was up as the first streaks of light showed in the sky, and decided to cycle to the riding school and explain to Felicity. She could look at the gate on the way. If Felicity, who would go straight there, found it off its hinges, she would replace it. Melanie wanted to see any evidence for herself.

She was wheeling her bicycle out of its shed when Paul walked along the path towards her.

'I didn't expect you to be up so early,' he said. 'Is all well?'

'Have you seen the ponies, and the lawns?' she asked. 'We had visitors during the night, that weren't scared off by Jim's dog! I haven't looked yet to see if they did any more damage. I'm going to try and find out how they got out of their paddock.'

'Be careful. I'll have a look round here while you're gone.'

The gate, when she got there, was not off the hinges, but the padlock swung loose, and Melanie saw that the chain had been snapped by an iron bar which lay unconcealed just beyond it. She left it, and when Felicity Grant, who owned the riding school, heard, she promptly rang the police.

'Criminal damage, and theft of my ponies, even if they did abandon them later. Mel, I'm so sorry! I'll get Des to stand guard by the gate. There may be fingerprints. Come on, I'll give you a lift back in the horsebox.'

They dropped off her husband, Des, to stand guard. Felicity saw that only three ponies were missing, and breathed a sigh of relief.

'If they'd left the gate open they could have been all over the village, causing mayhem. But it seems whoever it was had it in just for you.'

As they turned in through the gates of the Court, Paul flagged them down.

'Come and see what I've found,' he said.

They jumped down and followed him across the grass to the thick belt of evergreen bushes, laurels and rhododendrons, holly and viburnum, which bordered the lawns. He stopped and pointed. Melanie frowned. There were just a few scraps of something brightly coloured lying amongst last year's leaves. Felicity bent down to look.

'Balloons?' she asked thoughtfully. 'I see. They had them blown up, then punctured them to frighten the ponies once they'd got them inside your garden. There's three colours here, three balloons, at least. Leave them, and I'll send the police up here when they've been to see me.'

She loaded the ponies in the horsebox, refused breakfast, and drove off. Melanie wheeled her bicycle along the drive, thinking so deeply she did not at first hear what Paul said.

'I'm sorry, what was that?'

'The chain had been snapped, Felicity said. Could a woman have done that? Are we narrowing the suspects?'

'It wasn't a really big chain, I suppose. Felicity isn't concerned with theft of the ponies so much as preventing anyone letting them stray accidentally. With the leverage of that bar, a woman might have been able to break a link. I think I could have done.'

'There isn't much damage apart from the grass, and Jim and I have been trying to replace some of the divots. It won't look too bad, and it will have recovered completely by the June opening.'

'You're not having a very restful break,' Melanie apologised. 'I don't see why you should be dragged into my problems, but I'm very grateful.'

'I can't say it's a pleasure, but I'm glad to be able to help. Now go and have some breakfast. I'm hungry, too.'

For a moment, she was tempted to

ask him to join her in the kitchen, then bit the words back. He was a guest, paying her for his accommodation, but she was in danger of forgetting that. He'd become a friend, and she was tempted to lean on him for the kind of support she instinctively knew he'd provide. She mustn't let it happen.

She was trying to repair the grass towards lunchtime when Michael's Range Rover swept up the drive. He parked carelessly and leaped out, striding towards her with his arms held out.

'Mel, sweetheart, have you been attacked again?'

She allowed him to give her a swift hug, then drew back.

'What rumours did you hear this time, and how?'

'Someone in the village phoned Angela. You know how fast news gets round in Westford.'

'Angela? How did she come to tell you, even know you were here?'

He laughed. 'Angela, my sweet, was

more welcoming than you last night. She gave me a bed. After all, we were at school together.'

'Only just. You were several years ahead of her. It was Daniel in her year.'

'And I left before you got there. But she was very sympathetic to my plight.'

'You could have stayed if I'd had a room,' she reminded him.

'Have you a spare room tonight? I thought I'd take a few days off and stay to help you until this open week is finished. I can be an extra guard.'

Melanie sighed, knowing he'd be offended.

'I'm sorry, we're full until Tuesday. You can have a room Tuesday till Friday, but it's booked again after that.'

He frowned. 'How long is that Paul chap staying?'

'Until next Sunday.'

'OK, I'll fit in. I imagine Angela will let me stay until Tuesday. But I'll have to go back to London on Friday. Lots to do at the weekend. We miss you, Mel.'

She nodded.

'Now, please excuse me, I'm trying to repair as much as I can so that it doesn't look as if a troop of cavalry has been exercising here.'

'I thought you opened in the mornings, too.'

'Luckily the vicar objects, so it's afternoons only on Sundays. That gave us time to repair the worst of it.'

'Can you give me lunch? I'll help you. Then we're going out to dinner tonight. We need to talk, Mel.'

Suddenly, when she could least afford the time or energy, Mel thought, her social life was getting busy.

'We'd better eat here this evening,' she said. 'I'm too exhausted to eat out, and I might be needed if anything else happens,' she added hastily as she saw him open his mouth to protest.

He grinned. 'Not as private as I'd like! Now, is there anything I can do to help?'

'I don't think so. Paul and Jim have been doing this at the back,' she said, indicating the disturbed grass. 'It looked terrible to start with, but it's not so very bad. Paul has offered to roll it for me this afternoon, while I serve teas and chat. We can pretend work in the garden has to go on all the time, even on open days.'

'This Paul fellow, is he an old friend?'

'No. He's a guest, his first time here.'

Michael frowned. 'Then he's being remarkably self-sacrificing. Is he on his own?'

She could hear the slight tinge of jealousy in his voice, and recalled that when she had finally agreed to go out with him he'd expected her to refuse all other invitations. But they'd effectively split up when she'd decided to remain here after her father's death.

'Paul? Yes, he's here for a break, he said.'

'What does he do? Work, I mean. Odd place for a fellow to come for a break on his own.'

Melanie had thought this, too, but

she wasn't going to admit that to Michael.

'Come on, I'll fix us some lunch. I don't think any of the guests are staying in today, so Jane won't have anything prepared. Then I must get ready for the afternoon.'

'Your Paul not eating?'

'He said he'd go to the pub.'

She didn't add that he'd tried to persuade her to go, too, but she'd made the excuse there were things she had to do for the afternoon.

Jim was sitting at the table eating his lunch when they went indoors. Jane had soup simmering, and fresh rolls ready. Melanie mixed a salad and ate hungrily.

'Jim, you had no sleep last night. You should have been in bed this morning.'

'I can sleep the rest of the afternoon, Mel. Paul said he'd take over at two in the morning, so that I can go home and sleep before work tomorrow.'

'He mustn't do that! I think we ought to employ a night watchman. Do you know anyone who could do it?'

'One or two of the old lads in the village would be willing. I could leave Blackie with them.'

'I don't think you should use old-age pensioners, Mel,' Michael put in. 'It might be nasty, dangerous. Are you insured for this sort of thing?'

'Insured?'

Melanie looked at him in horror.

'For employees. Of course, if anyone offers to do it, and you don't pay them, that's different. It's their own look-out, but if they were hurt they might still try to sue you.'

'Well, I don't,' Jim said. 'What a thing! When we've all known Mel since she were a toddler.'

'That Paul fellow is a stranger. Yes, Mel, I know he's been kind and all that, but what do you know about him? If you were employing him, wouldn't you take up references?'

Melanie frowned. He was right in a way, and she hadn't thought about the insurance angle. She knew she could trust Paul, but no-one else would believe that. She had no basis for it except instinct and the fact that he'd been so kind.

'Shall I try to ring round for a proper security firm and see if we can get someone for tonight?' Michael asked. 'Jim looks tired out. He needs his sleep, and using a stranger, a guest at that, hardly seems fair to him. Why, you'd have to refund his money. You could hardly charge him for his food and board in the circumstances.'

'How much would it cost?' Melanie asked.

'I'll ring around and get quotes.'

5

When Michael emerged from her office an hour later, with various estimates, Melanie shook her head.

'No, I can't afford it. I'd never get it back.'

'You're doing this, maintaining the garden and hoping for the prize, out of sentiment,' Michael said. 'It's for your father, but he'd understand. He wouldn't want you to suffer all this worry just for the sake of a few pages in a glossy magazine. It's not as though you'd reap any benefit yourself, if you sell the house anyway.'

'I wish I could keep on the house, but Angela wants her share.'

'She could do with it now, I understand.'

'Has she been complaining to you?'

'No, but I do see her point. When she agreed to leave it for this year her husband was working, had a good job. They could afford to wait.'

'He has his redundancy. That should keep them going for this year, even if he can't get another job.'

'Mel, it's not just what she needs. I need you, too. You know that. Why don't you sell up and use your share to come in with me?'

'I'm not sure I want to go back to London. Westford is so different and I've come to appreciate it more these past few months.'

'Plenty of time for weekends in the country. We could buy another shop, you could manage it, and we could get married.'

'Married?' she asked. 'You didn't want to get married before.'

'No.' He raked his fingers through his hair. 'I didn't know how much I'd miss you when you left,' he admitted ruefully. 'Put the house on the market, before even worse damage is done, and come back to London with me.'

'I'll think about it.'

'Do you want a guard for the rest of this week?'

She shook her head.

'No, it costs too much. I'll leave it. We'll just try and stop them from getting in. I can lock the main gates, and block up the way in from the river. If someone hates me so much they bother to get past these, in order to ruin the garden, let them. Now I must go and open for the afternoon.'

Somewhat to her surprise, for she'd never seen Michael work in a garden before, he spent the afternoon doing all sorts of small jobs she hadn't had time for, and had left because they didn't affect the overall appearance of the garden. He also fetched a new fence panel and fixed it by the river to block that way in.

'They'll have to get wet if they try to come this way,' he said when Melanie went to inspect it. 'And I've stretched a wire under the water to trip them up if they try wading.'

They ate dinner in her office, efficient

with its computer, intercom and copier, but which was also a comfortable sitting-room. It even had french doors straight into the garden. Michael tried again to persuade her to give up. Melanie, knowing she was being stubborn and possibly unreasonable, insisted she meant to carry on.

She sent Jim, protesting, home late in the evening, and made Paul promise not to try and patrol the grounds during the night.

'You could be hurt,' she told them both. 'I don't want to be responsible for that.'

They accepted, reluctantly. Her decision seemed justified when nothing happened that night or the next, but on Tuesday night some of the upright posts of the pergola were sawn through and the entire roofing section had collapsed.

'It's wrecked!' she told Jane when she went back into the house. 'There's no way it can be repaired quickly.'

'They're so wicked!' Jane said.

'Don't cry, lass!'

'I'm not! I'm utterly furious! Why didn't I hear the sawing? Even though they used a hand saw I'd have thought I'd have heard something. I'm not sleeping too soundly lately!'

'There was a wind, a rough one, last night,' Jane said. 'That would cover the noise.'

'I can't find any traces of where they got in, and I've walked round all the boundary.'

'You can't make it a prison. They could have pushed through the hedges, or climbed the gate, even come in a small boat, one of those inflatables you can put in the back of a van.'

There was a knock on the kitchen door and Paul put his head round.

'Melanie, I heard. Susie told me. Is it possible to repair it?'

'Come in, Paul. No, too much damage. It would take at least a week to replace the posts and the top. But I'm not giving up!'

'Come on, let's go and see what can be done.'

As they picked their way across the fallen bars he took her hand, squeezing it comfortingly.

'Whoever did it must have been working for hours. He's ruined at least half the posts. Do you want to restore it eventually?'

'I'd like to, but is it worth the effort and expense?'

'If we took out the other posts it would look reasonable. You can call it the rose walk. Then, when this open week is done with you can replace the lot ready for the June opening, if you want to.'

Melanie nodded.

'That's the only thing to do, to make it look respectable.'

She suddenly realised he was still holding her hand. Embarrassed, she tried to pull away from him, but he laughed, and pulled her closer.

'Take a bit of comfort,' he said, and let go of her hand to put his arm round her shoulders and hug her.

For the first time since she'd discovered this latest damage, Melanie wanted to weep. She could manage to be angry, but this practical sympathy and offers of help made her feel weak. She took a deep breath and moved away.

'Let's start.'

They had taken away most of the debris, so that the path was clear by the time the gardens opened. Melanie had carted the last of the broken pieces of post to store them behind the hedge, and Paul was digging up the remaining posts when Michael appeared. Melanie heard him exclaim in anger.

'What the devil are you doing, Hunt? Is it you trying to wreck the garden?'

She didn't hear Paul's reply, and went back to try and explain, but before she could, Angela came running along the path from the house.

'Mel! What on earth's happened now? I came to see how you were and Jane told me.'

Melanie explained, while Paul calmly carried on dismantling the rest of the pergola.

'You'll have to give up now,' Angela said. 'It's getting dangerous as well as just spiteful.'

'I won't let them beat me! Apart from everything I need to know who could be so vicious.'

'You were always stubborn!' Angela snapped.

'Why don't you help me discover who it is instead of always criticising?' Melanie snapped, thoroughly fed-up with Angela. 'You could go round the gardens and talk to people, try and see how they react, if they look pleased to hear about what's happening here.'

'We could all do that,' Michael said, cutting off Angela's furious retort. 'Let's have lunch at the pub, and then you and Paul could go together, and Mel can come with me.'

'Good idea,' Paul said, just before Melanie was about to say she was busy enough here, and had no time for cosy meals at the pub. 'If you two can help us clear away these last few posts, we can clean up and be down there in half an hour.'

Melanie hid a grin as she registered Angela's look of dismay. Her sister wasn't dressed for rough garden work, in her smart trouser suit.

'If you can find me a broom, Angela, we can cart the rest away.'

Angela departed, while Paul carried on taking down the last few posts and Michael helped Melanie carry them away and store them in a neat pile behind the hedge. Soon they were walking down to the village pub.

They found a quiet table in a corner alcove, but it seemed as though everyone in the pub wanted to come and ask Melanie what had happened. They commiserated with her, but she thought she could see a certain excitement in their eyes, and some openly speculated on which of her rivals it might have been.

When they had all gone, Angela and

Michael mounted a combined attack, begging her to give up and sell now. Paul was mostly silent, just saying that it should be her decision, but if he were Melanie he'd want to discover the culprit. Michael looked at him in surprise.

'Are you a detective or a private eye?' he asked, and the sneer in his voice was evident.

'No, that's not my job.'

'What do you do?' Angela asked, turning a smile on him. 'Let's forget the garden for a few minutes. Tell us about yourself.'

'Oh, nothing interesting. I live in London, but I travel a lot for my firm.'

'What does your wife say to your being away?'

Melanie cringed. Did Angela have to be so blunt?

Paul looked at her calmly.

'I have no wife now.'

'Divorced? Oh, dear, how sad. I'm so sorry.'

'Angela,' Melanie began, but Paul

spoke at the same time.

'My wife died of cancer two years ago. She was pregnant with twins, but she died too soon for them to have a chance.'

Angela flushed.

'I'm sorry,' she muttered.

'What did your husband do?' Paul asked, and Melanie breathed a sigh of relief when Angela, still red with embarrassment, managed to reply.

Later, when Angela and Michael both ordered coffee Melanie refused, and stood up abruptly.

'I must get back. Thank you all for your help,' she said, and escaped before they could come with her.

She walked rapidly along the village street, ignoring everyone, silently fuming at the lack of moral support from her sister and her former boy-friend, and Angela's crass insensitivity towards Paul. How dared she ask him such personal questions!

Paul caught up with her and took her elbow in a friendly grip.

'Don't worry about them,' he said softly. 'The garden still looks terrific. I don't think the others can beat it. Besides, you have two more open weeks.'

'You mean nothing much else can go wrong?' Melanie asked, and gave a shaky laugh. 'Sorry I let you in for a family squabble, and Angela had no right to — '

'Don't worry. People are bound to wonder, a guy my age on his own. Will you be OK this afternoon? I thought I'd have another look round, visit the gardens I didn't get to before. I imagine you're too busy to come with me.'

'I have to be on hand some of the day,' Melanie said. 'People always want to ask questions. I just hope I know the answers. I'm a florist, not a hands-on gardener!'

'You do pretty well. If you're sure, I'll leave you here. But how about getting out of it tonight? We could have dinner again.'

'Thanks, I'd love that.'

And Michael could rage all he liked. She didn't belong to him, and had no intention of going into any sort of partnership with him, business or marriage, she thought as she walked the rest of the way home.

He didn't return until seven, and she met him on the stairs as she came down to meet Paul.

'You look great,' he said, stretching his hand across to the banisters and barring her way. 'That dress really shows your figure to advantage.'

This time she'd worn another of her London dresses, a tight-waisted, slim-skirted blue linen. She recalled that Michael had admired it when he'd seen her in it in London.

'I've found a passable restaurant and booked a table for half past seven,' he went on.

'I hope you enjoy it,' she replied. 'If you'll let me past I'll tell Jane you won't be in for dinner.'

'I'll go and change. Be with you in ten minutes.'

Melanie raised her eyebrows.

'But you surely can't expect me to come out with you after the attitude you're taking towards Paul. In any case, I have other plans.'

'Come on, Mel, we've been good together before, we can be again. You're upset because of all this garden thing. If you really want to carry on I'll be patient. So how about dinner tomorrow? It'll be my last night here, but I'll try to come down again in a few weeks.'

She bit her lip. Perhaps she did owe him some time alone, even if she doubted she could ever go back to working for him again, let alone anything closer.

'OK, tomorrow,' she said.

He leaned across and kissed her hard on the lips.

'That's my Mel. Enjoy yourself tonight.'

He released her and bounded up the stairs, almost colliding with Paul who was coming along the landing.

'Sorry, old chap. Take care of Mel

tonight. She's precious to me, as you'll have gathered.'

Melanie gave Paul a fleeting glance. He must have seen that kiss. Michael seemed intent on giving the impression he owned her, and she finally knew that she never wanted to be owned by him.

'I must have a word with Jane,' she murmured, unconsciously scrubbing at her lips as she went through into the kitchen.

Jane looked up from where she was preparing vegetables.

'Your lipstick's all smudged,' she said, and grinned. 'Which of your two swains was it?'

Melanie managed to laugh. 'You are an old romantic! Michael will be out for dinner. I don't know what he said before, but he's going out.'

She fished in her bag for her lip-gloss and repaired the damage.

'I feel guilty leaving you, in case something else happens.'

'Jim's here. Don't worry, Mel. Go

and enjoy yourself. That Mr Hunt's a real treasure.'

Paul had found another superb restaurant, ten miles away, behind one of the old inns in a small market town. Melanie hadn't known it existed. Briefly she wondered if he was someone who went round checking on restaurants for hotel guides.

To begin with, he told her which gardens he'd visited that afternoon, and what the owners had said about the troubles she was having.

'Everyone seems shocked and sympathetic,' he said. 'I didn't discover any secret satisfaction. They all seemed to wish you well.'

'That's what makes it so odd.'

'Let's forget it.'

Melanie was glad to, and they chatted about the history of the area, and which great houses and gardens were worth visiting.

'My wife loved tramping round castles,' he said suddenly.

'You must miss her dreadfully. I

didn't have time to say how sorry I was, when you told us.'

'It was hardly the time,' he said, and frowned. 'Yes, I'll always miss her, but she was in such pain it was a relief that she didn't have to bear it for too long. But it has been lonely without her. We were so looking forward to having children, too, though I have no idea if I'd ever have coped with twins on my own.'

'You'd have managed. People do. It must have been extra hard to lose them, too.'

'Yes, but I didn't know them like I knew Elizabeth. We had five years together, more than many people manage, when divorce is so common. At first I felt I could never look at another woman, but gradually I've come to realise that would be silly. One of the last things she said to me was that I must find another wife to ease the pain.'

'How wonderful of her. She wanted you to be happy.'

'Yes, but for a long time I didn't agree with her. Now, tell me about Michael. I gather he's rather more than a former boss.'

'We used to go out together,' Melanie explained. 'I think he's more interested in a business partnership now, using my money from the house, though the more I think of it, the more I want to keep on the Court and run it like Dad did. I'm going to look into what you suggested, a bank loan or mortgage. Maybe then I could pay off Angela, and Michael would see it's just not possible for us to work together.'

6

Michael departed, to Melanie's relief. Though she had agreed to have dinner with him it was, she insisted, for old times' sake. He brushed aside her repeated assertions that whatever happened, she would not be coming back to work for him, and had no interest in a partnership. Instead of listening to her, he described at length his own plans for expansion, how much she would benefit if she came in with him now, especially as a partner, and the attractions of the shop he hoped to buy.

'It's so close to lots of new office blocks, we could get the contracts for them before anyone else gets established. Then there are all the people working there, on good salaries. We could expand the functions aspect, do weddings and conferences.'

In the end, she had given in and

promised to consider it. It had seemed the only way to stop him bombarding her with demands to make up her mind.

'But I'm not promising anything, except to think about it, and I won't make any decision until after the June opening week,' she said at last.

Michael grinned.

'I think I can stall the people selling the shop for that long. You'll find it the best offer you ever had. And once it's established, Mel, we can think about getting married.'

Melanie lay in bed later, wondering why she had not been firm enough to turn him down properly. Delaying it served no purpose. She thought back over the conversation. Michael had taken her for granted. He had never mentioned that he loved her, and she seriously doubted that he ever had. She was a good florist, inventive and imaginative with her arrangements, and Michael knew she was an asset to his business. She felt sure it was that which made him so determined to get her back.

Now, of course, she had capital, or would have if she sold the house. If she ever put her share of that into the business it could easily double Michael's existing capital, and to him that would be a great attraction. The business earned well, but Michael spent lavishly. He had a good flat in a prestigious area, with a correspondingly large mortgage. He bought expensive cars and changed them every year.

He holidayed in luxury resorts, ate in the top restaurants, but spent little on expanding the business. Her money would be very useful to him, and a partnership would be a small price. No doubt he expected that, having once been her boss, he would still be able to make all the decisions without letting her have a say.

In June, she promised herself, she would make him understand they had no future, business or otherwise.

A few days later, Paul also left, but he

booked his room again for the open week in June.

'Nothing else has happened,' he said the evening before he left. 'Take what precautions you can without turning the Court into a fortress. Perhaps whoever it was has given up.'

Melanie felt bereft when he'd gone. To distract herself she began to make enquiries into the feasibility of bank loans and mortgages, and spent many evenings in her office calculating what she would need to earn to cover the repayments. Angela thought she was mad.

'I'd be glad of the cash,' she admitted a couple of weeks later, 'but you're crazy to consider taking on this barn. People only come in the summer, half the year. Dad made a decent living, but he didn't have a huge mortgage. And it must cost a lot to keep in good repair. With the prices you charge they want rooms renovated every couple of years, and that costs.'

'I know that. Dad used to redecorate

some rooms himself during the slack period, and I could do the same, but I was thinking of doing floristry, too. Jane and Susie can usually cope, so I could grow a lot of the flowers I'd need, send them out by post and do weddings. I could also run courses during the off season.'

'What sort of courses? Floristry? In the winter? Doesn't sound very attractive to me.'

'There's always flowers and greenery around. I could do Christmas decorations. It doesn't have to be floristry. There's cooking, painting, writing, computing, wine appreciation — all sorts of things. I could employ people to do those. There are several artists in the village who would probably appreciate earning a bit extra. Felicity might run riding courses, and maybe the golf club would put on events and people could stay here.'

'Too much fuss!'

'You and David might be able to lead some courses.'

Angela frowned, and then nodded slowly.

'It's possible.'

'Anyway, I'm making plans, and if I decide to go ahead I can start proper advertising after the June open week.'

'Susie tells me Paul Hunt's coming back then.'

'Yes,' Melanie replied, trying to sound nonchalant.

'Then why didn't he stay here last weekend?'

'Paul? Here? What do you mean?'

'I saw him in Westbridge on Friday, lunchtime.'

'Well, maybe he had business here, just for the day.'

'With Tom Harvey?'

Melanie frowned. 'What exactly did you see, Angela?'

'He and Tom were having lunch in The Three Pigeons. They were in that window table that looks out on to the High Street.'

'Perhaps they just ran into one another. He met Tom while he was going round the gardens.'

'Has Tom said anything to you?'

'I haven't seen him for ages, and why should he?' Melanie demanded angrily, getting tired of Angela's insinuations.

'Everyone in the village saw how attentive Paul Hunt was to you. Anyway, I spoke to Tom later in the afternoon. I ran into him an hour later, when I was coming back from the hairdresser. When I asked him if it had been Paul he looked shifty.'

'Shifty? Poor old Tom?' Melanie laughed. 'You're imagining it. But it's really none of your business, Angela. I expect Tom was embarrassed at being quizzed over whom he lunched with.'

'Maybe, but it took him a few moments to decide to admit it was Paul, and then he made an excuse about an appointment and almost ran away from me.'

'I'd have done the same.'

'Why don't you just sell up and take up Michael's offer?'

'Because I don't want to go into

partnership with Michael, nor do I want to marry him!'

'You don't know a good offer when it hits you in the face,' Angela said. 'I'm off.'

The following day, Michael rang to ask if it was true she had told her sister she was not going to marry him. Melanie clenched her hands into tight fists. How dare Angela interfere like this, first of all spying on her friends then reporting back to Michael their conversation!

'Since she has told you already, I can only repeat it. Thank you, Michael, but I've decided to stay here, so in the circumstances there can be no partnership, and no marriage.'

He protested, but eventually she ended the call, and tried to distract herself by making a list of the people who might be prepared to lead courses for her. She'd go and visit a couple right now and see how they reacted to the idea.

*   *   *

The next two months flew past. It was a particularly dry few weeks, and many of the plants would have suffered if Melanie had not been able to use domestic waste water to help them survive. Down by the river she could at first draw buckets of water from it, but it soon dwindled into little more than a trickle.

Angela was distant, especially after Melanie had had a blazing row with her about what she had told Michael. The sisters rarely saw one another, apart from a rather cool meeting at a birthday party for one of the children.

It was the afternoon Paul was due to arrive that Angela again came to the Court. She found Melanie dead-heading the roses, and admiring the newly-erected pergola.

'Has he got here yet?' Angela hissed, glancing round to make sure they could not be overheard.

'Who?' Melanie asked, determined

not to let her sister know she was aware whom Angela meant.

She'd been looking forward to Paul's arrival with a mixture of pleasurable anticipation and some anxiety. Apart from one e-mail to confirm his booking she had heard nothing from him since his previous visit.

'Paul Hunt, of course. As I came through the village I saw his car parked outside The Lodge. He'd be visiting Mrs Travers.'

'If you saw it there he can't have arrived here yet,' Melanie said. 'And how do you know it was his car?'

'I knew the registration number, and I didn't come straight here. I went to see Felicity to arrange riding lessons for the kids. I didn't realise they were so expensive. Have you sorted out a mortgage yet?'

Melanie shook her head. 'I'm waiting till after this next week.'

'Well, when you've finally made up your mind, do tell me. I'm rather tired of not being able to plan anything because you're shilly-shallying.'

'I'll arrange it this week,' she said, tight-lipped. 'It may take a few days for the money to be in the bank, but you'll have it as soon as possible. Do you want another valuation in case the house has gone up in the meantime, or will you accept the probate figure?'

'There's no need to be like that!'

'I'll get one done. After all, house prices could have gone down! Now excuse me, there's a lot to be done and I'm too busy to waste time arguing.'

Angela turned away, and Melanie watched her go back towards the drive, just as Paul's car swung along it. She wanted to drop her secateurs and basket and run to meet him, but not with Angela there, and not, when she remembered, after his silence over the past two months. Instead, she hurried along to the greenhouse and tried to busy herself potting up plants.

It was an hour later when Paul appeared in the doorway.

'Whew, it's hot in here! How are you,

Mel? I see the garden's looking better than ever.'

She smiled. She couldn't help it. She was so pleased to see him.

'Welcome back,' she said, and gasped as he stepped forward and enveloped her in a tight hug.

'It's good to be back. The roses are terrific, and I see you got the pergola replaced. Has there been any more trouble?'

'No,' Melanie said a little breathlessly.

It was such a warm day they were both wearing thin shirts, and she'd felt his heart beating strongly as he'd clasped her to his chest.

'Perhaps it's all over now. It could have been just a bit of spiteful vandalism. Are you busy, or can you have dinner with me tonight?'

'I — er — thank you. We don't have many guests until tomorrow, for the weekend.'

They went to the same restaurant where he'd taken her the first time. As they waited in the small bar the door opened and another couple came in.

'Why, Paul Hunt, and Melanie! What a lovely surprise. Darling, I told you about Mr Hunt. He was so appreciative of my garden and the way the landscape people had done it. Paul, this is my husband, John.'

'How do you do, Mr Seton-Woodward.'

'Are you all ready for the opening, Melanie?' Mrs Seton-Woodward asked. 'I don't know how you cope with such a large garden, so diverse, so many different areas. I must say I could only ever envisage something totally integrated. Just the one theme, you know, though I must say I'm getting a little tired of the classical, all those statues and temples and things. I am wondering if I should get it redone in the cottage-garden style. What do you think, Paul? Would it go with the house, have the right atmosphere?'

'The garden you have is less than a year old, I believe,' Paul said.

Melanie blinked in amazement. She stole a glance at Mr Seton-Woodward, and saw he was looking resigned. He noticed her glance and shrugged.

'It's Clarinda's hobby,' he said, almost apologetic. 'And no doubt it's cheaper to get it redone, and less upheaval, too, than to move house in order to find what we want.'

'Is that what you've done before?' Melanie couldn't help asking.

'A couple of times,' Mrs Seton-Woodward said, laughing. 'John's such a sweetie, indulging me. It's a good job he can afford it, isn't it?'

To Melanie's relief they were called to their table, and she restrained her giggles until they were out of earshot.

'Do you think she'll try to get it changed before the autumn open week?' she asked. 'Does she think she'll get extra marks for making a complete change? Doesn't the woman realise that gardens can change dramatically with the seasons?'

'The landscape people did it very

well,' Paul said, keeping his face deadpan.

Melanie chuckled. 'I imagine they'll have a job removing all that concrete and stone work.'

'She'll just have a bulldozer to shift it and a few tons of topsoil shipped in. Perhaps you should make a bid for the statues and the temple. You could lose them in your garden, behind the rhododendrons. Make it a Victorian folly if you dirty the stonework a bit.'

'No thanks!' Melanie said, and shuddered. 'I've nothing against statues, in their right place, which is not in a small village garden, or a large one like mine.'

'Yours?' he asked, smiling. 'Not your father's any more?'

Melanie shook her head. 'I've decided to keep it on. I can get a mortgage, just about, and I'm planning special events during the winter, to boost the occupancy rate.'

She told him her plans, and felt a

glow of satisfaction when he approved her ideas.

'That sounds enterprising. Can you cope, doing floristry and the garden, as well as the cooking?'

'I'll see. I can get someone in part-time when the garden needs more attention, if I am too busy doing other things.'

'And what does Michael say to these plans?'

She frowned. 'He's not happy, and we had a major row when I told him. But I don't want to go back to London, I don't want the partnership he's offering, and I don't want to marry him either.'

'I see.'

For the rest of the meal, they talked of other things. Paul had been in America for some weeks, though his only explanation was that he'd had to go for business, with no indication of what this was. He didn't mention having been in Westbridge and lunching with Tom Harvey, nor that he had called on Mrs Travers.

Melanie, wondering if she could ask him without appearing too possessive, recalled how well Mrs Seton-Woodward appeared to know him, after what she'd thought was just one visit to her garden. Was this just the natural effusiveness of the woman, or did he in some way know her better than she'd assumed? She decided she could not introduce the subject.

Eventually, after lingering over coffee and brandy, they set off for the Court. Melanie, after intensive days in the fresh air, was feeling sleepy, and sat up with a start when Paul suddenly accelerated and the car leaped forward, moving along the lanes at a dangerous speed.

'What is it?' she asked. 'Paul, what's the matter?'

'Can't you hear them?' he asked. 'Sirens of some sort, coming from the direction of Westford.'

Melanie could hear the faint noise now, and they were rapidly drawing nearer. She clutched the edge of the seat, praying they would not meet some emergency vehicle rushing towards them in the narrow lanes.

'It's OK, we're following them,' Paul said, as if sensing her nervousness.

They swept through the village and into the lane leading up to the Court. As the powerful car swung through the gates and slewed to a halt behind two fire engines, Melanie cried out in dismay. Beyond the house, smoke billowed up in dense black clouds, and flames licked the tinder-dry hedges.

7

Melanie was out of the car before Paul switched off the engine, and running towards the back of the house. It was still light enough to see that part of the orchard, close to the river, and the lawn in front, had been blackened, and the hedge alongside was still on fire.

'Steady, miss, don't go any nearer,' one of the firemen said, stretching an arm across to hold her back.

'No. How long has it been burning?' she asked, straining to see what the damage was.

'We got here half an hour ago. The grass was tinder dry, and it had spread to the hedge. The trees have suffered, I'm afraid, but it's all under control now.'

'It's burned fiercer than normal,' another man put in. 'I can smell petrol, and I'll bet you anything this was started deliberately.'

Melanie groaned. 'Not again! I can't bear it if this all starts again!'

At that moment, Paul reached her, and a police car drew up in the drive. Two uniformed policemen got out and walked across.

'Come inside, Mel, you're shivering,' Paul said, putting his arm round her and pulling her close to him. 'There's nothing you can do here.'

'Yes, go in, Miss Hetherington,' one of the policemen said. 'We'll come and talk to you when we've heard what the firemen have to say.'

With a last look round at the ruins of this part of the garden, she turned away and went inside. Jane and Susie were standing in the conservatory doorway, watching, and Jane exclaimed as she saw Melanie.

'Come in, Mel, and I'll make a pot of tea. I should think the firemen could do with one, too.'

They went into the kitchen where Jim was sitting by the table, and Jane busied herself with the kettle.

'When did it start?' Melanie asked.

'Mr Collins, in Room Six, saw it when he went up after dinner,' Jane said.

Susie nodded.

'He said he was standing in his bedroom window admiring the view when he saw smoke, and then the flames seemed to shoot across the corner of the garden. He rang for the fire brigade from his mobile, before he came down to tell us. I was in the bar, but we all went out to see if we could do anything.'

'We couldn't get near,' Jim said, 'and anyway the water pressure on the hose is so low we could only keep it on the surrounding area to try and stop the fire spreading.'

'The jealous gardener strikes again,' Susie said.

'Hush, girl, you can't know,' Jane said, frowning at her.

'It might have been an accident,' Jim said. 'Lord knows, there's been little enough rain and the ground's parched.'

'The firemen seem to think it was started with petrol,' Melanie said, accepting a mug of tea from Jane. 'Thanks. Could you smell petrol, Jim, when you were out there?'

He thought for a moment. 'I might have. It's difficult to tell, I'm surrounded by petrol fumes at work all day.'

'If they used petrol it's no accident. Mel, what can we do?' Jane asked. 'When it was just silly tricks it was annoying, but it could be put right. This is dangerous.'

Melanie nodded. 'I know, Jane, but who would go to these lengths to win a competition? Surely no-one else in Westford would do this to me just to ruin my chances of the prize.'

'It's not even certain you would get it,' Susie put in. 'Tom Harvey's garden is pretty spectacular this year, and there are one or two others in the running. I hear that even that Mrs

Seton-Woodward has been getting good marks.'

Jim grunted. 'But that's from townies who don't know what a garden should look like, and go for showy stonework!'

'Mrs Seton-Woodward was in the same restaurant as we were tonight,' Melanie said, 'and in any case I can't imagine her crawling round with cans of petrol setting fire to my garden.'

'Has anyone else got a grudge against you?' Paul, who had been silent until now, asked.

'It's rather frightening to think I may have enemies who'd go to these lengths,' Melanie said, shuddering.

It was several hours later before she crawled into bed. She'd had to talk to the firemen, who promised to come back and make more tests in the morning.

'It's all damped down now, safe to leave it,' they assured her.

'That may be, but I'm keeping watch if you don't leave someone,' Jim said.

Then Melanie had to talk to the

police, who said they were almost certain it had been arson.

'We'll be looking into it, but it's dark now. We'll be back in the morning.'

'And what's my garden going to look like with firemen and police all over it, apart from the mess?' Melanie said. 'Is it worth opening?'

'Surely you're not going to give up now, let whoever it is win,' Paul said, and Melanie straightened her shoulders.

'Of course I'm not! Though my chances seem to be diminishing by the day! I wonder what else will happen.'

Unable to sleep, she tried to put herself into the shoes of whoever her enemy was, and try to imagine what other tricks they might play. The greenhouse was vulnerable. Either the heating system or the glass could be attacked, but breaking glass would be noisy. They'd risk being heard and caught. No heating was required now, and though interfering with it so that it needed repair could be expensive, it would have little effect on the garden display.

The flowers and shrubs might be cut down. That could be done secretly at night, and would be more obvious, spoiling the display. Ought she to hire a guard, and forget the expense?

It was nine in the morning when Susie brought her breakfast in bed.

'Room service, Mel,' she sang out, and Melanie dragged herself from the sleep which had finally come a few short hours earlier.

'Susie? What's this?'

'Mum said you were to take it easy, not to hurry, but the police will be here in an hour or two, and you'll want to talk to them. Mr Hunt's gone out straight after breakfast, in his car.'

'Did you get any sleep? You were up late, too,' Melanie said, and yawned.

'We went to bed when the police were talking to you. Don't you remember? You sent us all off, all but Mr Hunt.'

'I must see Mr Collins, too, and

thank him. If he hadn't seen it we might have had more damage.'

The rest of the morning was taken up by the police, the firemen and the newly-arriving visitors, as well as several villagers who called to find out what had happened, or asked if there was anything they could do to help. Melanie discovered how much she was missing Paul. She longed for him to be there, to talk things over with, to test out her ideas of how she could overcome this latest disaster.

It had been arson. There was no doubt of that. The police found that the fence Michael had put up earlier did not now extend into the river, it was so low. Besides, they found the indentations made by feet in the mud at the edge of the water.

'A common trainer pattern,' one of the policemen said. 'All we can do is take a mould and if we ever find a match it would be suspicious, but not definite proof.'

'What we think happened,' one of the

firemen explained, 'was that he got over to the hedge sheltered by the shrubs farther up the garden. Then he poured petrol over the hedges, and scattered some over the grass on the way back down to the riverbank. He could set light to it there and get away before the flames spread and could be noticed. This sloping bit of the orchard's out of sight of the house even if anyone were to be looking.'

'I see.'

It didn't help, Melanie thought, knowing how it had been done. What she desperately wanted to know was who had done it.

Jim had been busy fencing off the damaged section of the garden.

'It won't look too bad, Mel,' he said when she was snatching a sandwich at lunchtime, but she knew he was trying to console her. 'It looks terrible now, but it's only a smallish section, and it's in the corner. It won't look too odd to people who don't know the garden at all.'

'I know, and you've all been so good.'

Where was Paul, she wondered, but she had to set aside thoughts of him and talk to visitors, telling them they'd had a small fire the previous day, and that explained the smell of smoke, and the dampness on the grass near the new fence. Whether or not news of the fire had spread farther than the village, Melanie didn't know, but she seemed to have more visitors than normal.

By the time they closed, and the last visitor had left, it was seven, and Paul had still not returned. Melanie decided she'd have some supper, do some paperwork, and have an early night; try to catch up on the loss of sleep.

She was in the kitchen a couple of hours later, having decided to do her accounts at the table there, partly for company, partly so that she could keep an eye on the garden, when Paul and another man walked in through the back door. Melanie bit back her question of where had he been all day. She had no right to ask that, just because he was kind and she felt at ease with him.

'Melanie, this is Jason Fletcher, a pal of mine. He's your new night watchman.'

'Evening, miss,' he said, his voice deep and sonorous.

Jason Fletcher was large in every way. Tall, broad-shouldered, barrel-chested, with enormous feet and hands, he seemed to fill the kitchen. Susie, coming in from the dining-room with a tray of used glasses, gaped at him, and Melanie bit back a giggle.

'I decided it was too much hassle to hire anyone,' she said, 'especially with insurance complications.'

'Don't concern yourself, miss,' Jason said. 'I run my own security firm. I'm insured, and I've got a couple of big guard dogs. No-one will get past them or me.'

'But how much do you cost?'

Melanie was trying to work out in her

head what this would do to her profits and her cash flow once she had the mortgage sorted.

Jason looked disconcerted, and glanced across at Paul.

'Don't worry, Melanie, I'm paying Jason,' Paul said. 'He — er — owes me a favour, don't you, Jason?'

'Oh, yes, of course. Well, I might as well start.'

'And I'll take over while Jason has a break, around midnight,' Paul said. 'If you could leave him a few sandwiches and a flask of coffee, can he come in here?'

'I'll get a couple of extra loaves for your sandwiches,' Susie said, and giggled. 'You look as though you need a lot of fuel to keep you going. Can I feel your biceps?'

'Susie,' Melanie protested. 'Paul, I can't let you pay!'

'You've no choice, it's already agreed. Jason's here for the rest of the week. And there's a room at the Three Crowns for him.'

She was too tired, and if she admitted it, too thankful, to argue. She'd be able to sleep in peace.

'Go to bed, you look whacked. I'll show Jason round.'

'Thanks, Paul, and Jason. Goodnight.'

She stood for a while at her bedroom window, and saw Jason walking slowly round the garden. His two dogs, long, sinuous shapes in the dusk, roamed back and forth. No-one would want to challenge them!

She woke refreshed at her usual time of six, and took a long, hot shower. In the kitchen she found Jason sitting by the table, nursing a mug of tea. Jane was cooking in the largest frying pan they possessed. Jason made to rise when she went in, but she waved him back.

'Don't get up. Was everything quiet?'

'Sure, just a few rabbits and a fox which tried to cross the river, but one look at my Bill and Ben and they high-tailed it.'

'Where are the dogs?' Melanie asked, looking round the kitchen a little apprehensively.

'Outside, patrolling. Don't worry, they won't harm anyone. They've been trained to hold them until I get there. I'll be out again in ten minutes, before you're likely to get visitors.'

He was proved wrong two minutes later, when a woman's screams sent them all rushing outside. Angela was cowering against her car, staring at one of the dogs which stood a yard away from her. The other paced up and down a yard farther back. Melanie felt like laughing. With all the grief Angela had been giving her the past few months, over selling the house, and Michael, Melanie enjoyed seeing her sister flustered for once.

Jason uttered a soft command, and the dogs immediately came to him. He patted them, murmured a soft endearment, and smiled across at Angela.

'It's all right, ma'am, they won't hurt you.'

Angela glared at him, and burst into speech.

'Mel, what the devil's this? Can't I come and see my sister without being attacked by these great vicious brutes?'

'They don't seem vicious to me,' Melanie said. 'This is Jason Fletcher. Jason, my sister, Angela Constantine. And I don't know which of the dogs is Bill or Ben,' she finished, suppressing a giggle.

Angela glared at her.

'Am I allowed to come in? You seem to have turned the Court into a fortress.'

'Haven't you heard about the fire?' Melanie asked, leading the way back into the kitchen.

Angela usually heard of what happened in Westford before the locals did.

'Fire? What fire? I've been away for a couple of days. We went to Penzance to see David's parents. They've just got back from Canada, visiting his sister. I wish we could afford to go to Canada.

A couple of days at Blackpool will be all we can manage this year.'

Seeing Jane still preparing Jason's breakfast, Melanie led the way through to her office. She called Susie over the intercom, asking her to bring them some coffee and toast when she had a minute.

'Have you had breakfast? Why are you here so early?'

Angela sighed.

'I was hoping his parents would be able to lend us some cash. This dry weather's opened up some cracks in the house, and the bill for repairs is horrendous. We'd be able to pay them back when you've sold here. But they said they didn't have anything to spare, even for a short loan. So we decided to drive back overnight. The children always sleep in the car on motorways, anyway. I came to see how things are going, whether you've got the mortgage sorted out yet.'

'I will do soon, unless there are any complications because of the fire.'

Melanie explained, and rather grimly noticed that Angela's only concern was how it might affect the value of the property and her share of it.

'Will they try to reduce the mortgage, or say you're a bad risk?' she asked.

'I have no idea. I'll get on to them on Monday and let you know as soon as I hear.'

'Thanks, Mel. Who is that gorilla out there, by the way, with his mean-looking hounds?'

'He's a friend of Paul's, runs his own security service, and he's doing watchman duty for the rest of this week. I'm very grateful to him.'

'Well, I'm not sharing the cost!'

'I haven't asked you to.'

Melanie didn't feel like explaining that Paul was paying for it.

'It's only because you want to keep the garden that it's necessary,' Angela began to say, for once sounding apologetic, but Melanie waved her to silence.

'Forget it. Oh, Susie, come in. Thanks. Angela, if you've driven all the way from Penzance you must be starving. Have some coffee?'

8

To Melanie's great relief, nothing more happened that week. Paul took her out a couple of times, but she was very busy with the many visitors, and also trying to clear the burned area of garden and decide what was the best thing to do with it.

Tom Harvey had come over to see her, and they walked round the garden together.

'The hedge will probably regenerate next year as it wasn't completely burnt. The damage was mainly at the top, where the petrol was thrown on. You could wait, or try to replace it. Who could have been so malicious?'

'Everyone thinks it's a rival for the prize,' Melanie told him.

She could not believe her father's old friend could be so devious.

'Me, you mean?' he asked, and

chuckled. 'Well, if I win, there'll be some who say I did it. But from what I've seen, the garden's better than ever. You'll win on merit, never mind what's been done to spoil it for you.'

'Thanks, Tom. I never believed it was you.'

He gave her an abstracted smile.

'Your dad wasn't himself last year. You've tidied it up a treat. I think he was worse, sicker than he let on to any of us. He didn't seem to have the same energy as before.'

'I wish I'd spent more time with him.'

'You couldn't have guessed. None of us knew, and we saw him almost every day. Angela came over every week, too.'

It was two days after Paul left, booking once more for the autumn opening three months ahead, that Angela appeared one morning.

'Mel, I have to talk to you.'

'If it's about the mortgage, the money should be available by the end of the week.'

120

'Oh, that's good, but it wasn't about that.'

Melanie raised her eyebrows. It had been almost the only thing Angela had been interested in the past few months.

'So what is so serious to bring you over like this?'

'You know my friend, Nita, works for the estate agency in the High Street.'

'Yes?' Melanie asked suspiciously.

'Guess who was in there last week, asking to be kept informed if the Court was put on the market?'

'But I'm not going to sell.'

'You've made that perfectly clear. It was your friend, Paul Hunt. It gave me an idea. He's been in cahoots with all your main rivals, which is suspicious, but suppose he's just using the pretence of rival gardeners to throw us off the scent?'

'The scent of what? Do get to the point, Angela. I have lots to be getting on with.'

'Your precious Paul Hunt, this mysterious man who turns up out of nowhere, and won't tell us what he does for a living, could be trying to drive down the value of the Court before he buys it.'

'Buys it? But he knows I'm not selling!'

'Why should he want to know the value, and to be kept informed if you do? Who knows, much more of this vandalism and you might decide to give in.'

'Are you suggesting he did any of the damage? But we were out together the night of the fire.'

'The Jubilee garden prize could be just a smokescreen, and we know he has an accomplice. What better alibi than to be out with you when things happen? Jason could have set the fire.'

'You're blaming him just because his dogs frightened you. I don't believe either he or Paul could be crooks. That's what you're suggesting.'

'What I think he is, Paul, I mean, is a property developer.'

'Oh, this is pure guesswork! Just

because the man talked to an estate agent.'

'Why do that if he's not interested? My guess is he wants to buy the Court cheaply, then he could convert it into flats.'

'It wouldn't be allowed!'

All the same, Melanie felt a frisson of fear. How could she bear it if her lovely home was divided up, sold off to people who wouldn't care about it? And what would she do, where could she go?

'I'm not going to sell,' she insisted.

'You might have to, if you can't make it pay with all your schemes.'

Melanie nodded reluctantly.

'I know, and it will be hard work, but I'm going to do my best to make it pay.'

'If you don't, you'll have to sell. It's a good investment for someone who has the money and know-how to develop it.'

Maybe, if the worst happened, she could do that herself, Melanie thought, and then shook her head. How would she ever raise the necessary cash?

Angela was still talking.

'There's plenty of land, and I've asked at the council offices. He could stand a good chance of getting planning permission. He'd make a fortune. Look at the price of those houses Mrs Seton-what's-it lives in. He could build a dozen more like that as well as get half a dozen apartments in the house itself.'

She didn't believe Paul could be so devious. Everything that had happened had been connected with the garden, attempts to ruin her chances for the competition. Nothing else made sense.

'Michael rang to ask how you were,' Angela said after a slight pause. 'He's still fond of you, and you could do a lot worse than him.'

'I didn't know you two were such buddies.'

'I knew Daniel better when we were in the same year at school, and it was through Daniel that you were introduced to Michael when you wanted a job as a florist.'

'Sure, but why does he ring you and not me?'

'He doesn't want to ring you. You might just put the phone down, but he's very upset. He asked me to tell you he was willing to wait until the end of the year, after the last garden opening, if you'll change your mind.'

'I won't. Please tell him so.'

'If that's what you want.' She rose to go. 'Mel, why can't we be friends again like we used to be? This silly competition has come between us.'

'I know, and I'm sorry!' Melanie said, and they hugged.

'Good. Oh, I almost forgot. It's James's birthday at the end of July, and he wants a garden party. Will you come?'

Melanie thought of Angela's tiny garden, and a dozen or more boisterous six-year-olds rampaging round it. She recalled the wonderful parties she and Angela had enjoyed here at the Court, with room to run about, a few easy trees to climb, swings and rope ladders hanging from branches. The old tree house was probably still useable.

'Would you like to have it here?' she asked abruptly, before she could have second thoughts.

Angela looked at her for a moment.

'Mel, that would be wonderful. Do you really mean it?'

'Of course I do. And we'll make him a cake if you can get the rest of the food. You know what that age likes better than I do.'

'Fabulous! Jane's a dab hand at fancy cakes for kids. Could she do a train, do you think? I know that's what he'd like.'

Later Melanie wondered if she'd been rash, but she was committed. Jim checked the tree house, replaced the ropes, and Jane, saying she rarely had the chance to do cakes for boys, spent her spare moments studying pictures of Thomas the Tank Engine and his friends.

The day of the birthday dawned clear and warm, removing Melanie's last worry. Angela and her family were to be here at two, to get ready, and the other children were coming at three.

★   ★   ★

The last of the parents had driven away, and David was trying to organise a game, when Melanie saw a Range Rover turn in through the gates. She froze, and hastily counted the children, wondering if there was still one to come. Then she watched in mounting irritation as Michael jumped down from the car and walked across to her. How could Angela have taken advantage of her in such a way! Michael looked at her, doubt in his eyes.

'Hello, Mel.'

'What brings you here?' she demanded, her tone uncompromising.

'Please, can we talk? I've had some ideas, ways we can compromise. But we can't talk here,' he added, glancing irritably at the stream of exuberant children racing around them, screaming at the tops of their voices.

Melanie was developing a headache from the noise and tension.

'Come in, then.'

They walked back to the house, leaving Angela and David and a couple of the mums to cope. Jane, doing last-minute things to the train cake, glanced at them as they passed through the kitchen.

'I'll bring you some tea,' she said. 'Your office?'

'Thanks.' Melanie smiled at her.

She and Michael sat down in facing armchairs, and Melanie closed her eyes, breathing deeply as she tried to ward off the pain.

'Mel, are you OK?' Michael asked.

'Headache. I'll be fine in a minute. I'm not used to kids and the sheer volume of noise they can make.'

Jane came in with a tray, and stayed to pour two cups of tea.

'Here, a couple of aspirin. Take them.'

Melanie smiled her thanks, swallowed her tablets, and when Jane had gone, turned to Michael.

'I meant what I said the last time. I have no intention of selling up here, and I don't want a partnership, flattered though I am that you've offered me one.'

He nodded, and smiled.

'I believe you've taken on a huge mortgage so that you could buy Angela out.'

'Did she tell you that? She's no right to talk about my affairs!'

'No, no,' he said hastily. 'She just said she'd soon have the money from the house, and as you aren't selling, it's the only possible solution. But it will be a terrific strain on you. Look at this headache. You never used to have headaches.'

'This one isn't due to any difficulties with the house!' Melanie said, irritated. 'It was the sudden noise of the children.'

'Yes, of course. But I suspect the underlying worry is a part of it, making you more vulnerable.'

'Are you a doctor now, or maybe a psychiatrist? Michael, come to the point. What is it you came here to say?'

He took a deep breath and glanced round the room.

'Nice room you have. Cosy, big enough for two.'

'What on earth do you mean?'

'Mel, if the mountain won't move — you know the rest. I've been thinking hard. If you're determined to stay here, why don't I leave London and move here? No, wait,' he hurried on as she opened her mouth to speak. 'Don't dismiss it out of hand. I can leave a manager in London, go up once a week perhaps, and we could be partners here. If I sell my flat I could put in as much as your mortgage, and we could open a shop in Westbridge, too. Angela tells me there's no-one in the area who can do what we could offer.'

Melanie stared at him, bemused.

'You don't own your flat. By the time you've paid off the mortgage on it, and the fees, I doubt you'd have enough for more than a new shop. You couldn't have enough to pay off my mortgage, too.'

'Property values in London have soared. You'd be surprised. We could manage a small mortgage. We could employ a proper chef here, get a real reputation for good, healthy country food. It's all the rage now, using local produce. We could grow a lot of it, have our own chickens — '

'Wait!' Melanie found her voice. 'I'll never get rid of Jane! She cooks as well as any four-star chef!'

'I'm not suggesting we get rid of her, but there are other jobs she could do. You've got space here for a bigger dining-room. We could have a restaurant, and in time build an annex for more bedrooms. It could be a gold-mine!'

'It was my home and I don't want those sort of changes.'

Her headache, which had begun to recede, now came back with full force. She had to get rid of him.

'Michael, I appreciate how much thought you've put into this, but you've forgotten one thing. I don't want to get married.'

He looked downcast for a moment, then rallied.

'We could be just business partners. We worked well together before, didn't we?'

When he was the boss and she a humble employee! Melanie strongly suspected that he was contemplating the same relationship should he ever join her here. She rubbed her forehead.

'Michael, I'll think about it, OK? Now, please, my head's splitting. I have to lie down. Go and help Angela with her kids.'

Eventually, when she'd promised to give him an answer by the end of the month, in just over a week's time, he left, and her headache immediately began to get better. She took the tray back to the kitchen, told Jane she was going to lie down for a while, and escaped to the sanctuary of her room.

She knew the answer without further thought. In London, Michael had been amusing, exciting, and she'd thought she loved him, but in the time she'd spent back here she'd discovered she didn't really want a big-city life. Nor did she want the big-city style introduced here. Michael's ideas would change all that. Change, or constant argument would be the result if she agreed to his plan.

Nor, she thought, did she even doubt if she loved him now. She had sometimes thought it was her unrelenting hard work in the first few months which had made her think of him only rarely. Now she knew she hadn't missed him, not really. He wasn't essential to her.

A picture of Paul Hunt floated into her mind. Why didn't he keep in touch in between his visits? And would the visits end after the garden opening weeks? There was only one more, at the end of September. Why did he come specially at those times? He seemed to appreciate gardens, but he didn't know a great deal about them, she'd concluded.

She wondered if she had fallen in love with Paul. He was attractive, unattached, had suffered pain with the loss of his wife. He gave practical help, not ambitious and controversial suggestions. She was certain it had been the presence of Jason which had prevented more attacks on her garden in June.

Should she contact him? She could send a friendly letter perhaps. Then she recalled Angela's information about the enquiries he'd been making at the estate agents. Even Paul had secrets, and they seemed to be connected in some way with the Court. She didn't know what he did for a living. He was well off, with his new registration car. Many property developers were well off, she knew. Some, she'd heard, would wait years for the best time to take their profits.

She was trying to work it all out as she fell asleep, to be wakened an hour later by Angela shaking her shoulder.

'Mel? Jane said you were feeling rotten. I'm so sorry. The kids are having tea now, and James 'specially asked me to get you to see him blow out the candles. Do you feel fit enough?'

'Has Michael gone?'

'Yes, he left right after he'd been talking to you.' Angela gave her a searching look. 'I'm so hoping you'll make it up with him. He looked cheerful enough, anyway.'

'Give me ten minutes. My headache's gone. I'll have a quick shower to freshen up, and be down.'

To her relief, the rest of the party was much quieter, with a friend of David's giving the children a puppet show, and soon even Angela and her family had departed.

'Your cake was a great success, Jane,' Melanie said as she helped clear up and prepare for the guests' dinner.

'Young James is a nice lad, but I'd love to have your children to bake birthday cakes for, Mel.'

Melanie forced a laugh.

'Well, don't look to Michael to provide them!'

She told Jane what Michael had suggested, and held up her hand in surrender when Jane protested.

'Don't worry. I never want to change the Court, not in that way, at least. And I'd never dream of replacing you with some fancy chef. But it was a good idea to grow some of our food, and fresh eggs would be great.'

Jane nodded. 'Your dad said he didn't have the time, but you could perhaps turn that burnt area into a vegetable patch. It's out of sight, you could plant all round with a thick hedge, replace the old one. That would give protection as well as screening.'

'I'll organise something next week,' Melanie responded.

She put aside the idea of writing to Paul, but she composed a careful letter to Michael. In it she explained she'd given his ideas a good deal of thought, but concluded that it would not work to have a partnership when they had such radically different ideas. She said she'd enjoyed working with him in London, and had at one time thought they might have a closer personal relationship, but she had concluded they were too different for that to work.

If she'd loved him, it might have been different, but she'd discovered she could feel no more than friendship, and for her that was not enough for marriage. She did not think it would ever change. And just to try and stop him pursuing it, she hinted there was someone else, a man she knew in Westford, for whom she had warmer feelings.

'That should stop him,' she murmured as she sealed the envelope.

She'd post it straight away, at the village shop.

Susie was at Reception sorting through the day's post when she went to head off.

'Looks like more bookings for your courses, Mel,' she said, waving a handful of letters. 'I think most of them have enough people coming to break even, after you've paid the tutors.'

'Good. I'll look at them when I get back.'

'Here's one marked personal.'

Melanie's heart gave a sudden leap. Was it from Paul? Then she chided herself for being silly. Just because she'd been thinking of him didn't mean he'd written. She took the letter and saw the address was typed. As she walked towards the front door, she ripped it open and pulled out the single sheet, then stopped dead as she saw the headed notepaper. She read the letter hastily, then sat down and read it more carefully, ignoring Susie's anxious demands to know if she was all right.

We are occasionally approached by potential purchasers who have seen and much desire particular properties, she read, *and even though we have no reason to believe the owners have any intention of selling we feel bound to pass on these offers. We have received* an enquiry about Westford Court, and an offer substantially above that of the probate valuation, which as you are aware we carried out. If you are interested, and we have to point out that it is far more than you would be likely to obtain on the open market, please contact me at the above address.

9

Melanie went straight into Westbridge, to ask the estate agent who their client was. She was dreading that it might be Paul. Until now she had barely realised how much it meant to her to know for certain he was not taking her for a ride, coming here and pretending to help, while trying to drive down the price of the house, or make her so scared she'd jump at the first chance to sell it.

When Angela had first suggested something of the kind, she'd brushed it aside as impossible. Insidiously, though, the odd questions kept coming into her mind. Why had he been talking to the other gardeners? He'd met them during the first open week, in fact could have spent lots of time with them if he'd wanted, so why these other visits?

He would not try to ruin her garden, though. She could not believe that of him. He knew how much it meant to her, not so much winning the prize, but keeping up the garden in memory of her father.

Angela's friend, Nita, who'd been in her class at school and had often visited the Court, was at the front desk when Melanie walked into the office.

'Hello, Melanie.'

'Nita, what do you know about this?' Melanie thrust the letter in front of her. 'Who is it?'

Nita shook her head.

'I don't know, honestly, Melanie. One of the partners deals with this sort of thing.'

'Then I'd better see whoever wrote it.'

'It's Mr Chamberlain. I'll ask if he's free.'

A few minutes later, Melanie was shown into an inner office, where a large, brawny-looking man rose from his desk to usher her to a seat opposite. She explained that Westford Court was not for sale, and asked to know who was interested, so much so they were offering a ridiculous price.

'Well, my dear,' he began, 'in the first place, it's a good position, a thriving business, and values have been going up in the area.'

'But you said not to this extent. Who is this person?'

'I'm afraid I can't say. Client confidentiality, you know.'

'Is it someone who wants to develop it, perhaps build more houses, and is hoping to make a huge profit out of it without my knowing?'

He shook his head, smiling condescendingly.

'Now, now, you know I can't comment on that. If we did sell to this client, however, they would pay all the fees. We would not charge you any, since you did not initiate the sale.'

Melanie could bear it no longer. She was clearly not going to discover who it was. She stood up abruptly.

'Mr Chamberlain, tell your client I have no intention of selling Westford

Court, whatever the inducements — or threats — and if I ever do sell, it will not be through your agency. Good morning.'

She had still not simmered down when she got back to Westford, and instead of going home, she called on Tom Harvey. She could trust him, surely. He was in the garden, and smiled at her as she walked through the gate.

'Come in, Melanie. You look flushed. How about a glass of something cold? Lager or Coke?'

'Coke, please. That would be good.'

When they were sitting under the shade of a horse chestnut at the end of Tom's garden, Melanie told him about the letter.

'Am I being paranoid, or could all these attacks be connected? Might it be someone wanting to get my land for building? Someone trying to frighten me away?'

Tom looked shocked. 'Surely no-one could be so devious!'

'But could they build there? Would they get planning permission? Tom, you're on the parish council, you know something about all this.'

'Well, it depends, but with all the pressure to build more houses, and the fact Westford isn't protected in any way, it's not a conservation area, for instance, more building could be allowed.'

'So it might be a property developer. Tom, Angela once saw you having lunch with Paul Hunt, at the Three Pigeons. She thought there was something secretive about it.'

'That was months ago, soon after he first came here. We met by chance in the High Street in Westford. Why?'

'I'm wondering about him. He's been here both open weeks, and is coming again. Why should he do that? What's his interest in Westford? Why should he come down in between? Why did he visit Mrs Seton-Woodward, and Mrs Travers? He's never mentioned that to me, and I thought we were friends, he was so helpful when all the trouble started, and he got Jason down here as a night-watchman. What did you talk about that day you met him?'

Tom shook his head. 'Mainly about the Jubilee prize, how it had been set up. You can't suspect him of doing any of the damage, surely?'

'I hope he didn't, but I know nothing about him, what he does, why he comes here, and Angela said he'd been asking to be told if the Court were ever put up for sale. Nita, her friend, told her.'

'Nita shouldn't be gossiping about her employer's business. What is it you're afraid of?'

'Is Paul a property developer? He's rich enough to afford a luxury car, he's interested in the Court if it's for sale, and he may be trying, very deviously, to drive me into selling.'

'If he is, why should he make an offer now?'

'Perhaps he thinks someone else is after it. But why does he talk to Mrs Travers and Mrs Seton-Woodward, and never mention it to me?'

'I may have suggested Mrs Travers would be able to tell him about the hospice. He seemed very interested in that aspect. Her sister was there, you know, until she died. Of course,' he mused almost to himself, 'she was saying all sorts of things, slanderous, some of them, the first few months, claiming they hadn't offered her sister treatment that might have cured her, and that she was not going to help raise funds for them any more. But she came round when we asked her to be on the committee.'

'Vandalising my garden hardly fits in with that.'

'Mr Seton-Woodward is a builder, of course.'

'What?'

Melanie felt her head begin to spin.

'Yes, he built all those new houses, as well as the one for himself. He has pots of money, from what I've heard.'

'Could he be after the Court? Could his wife want to live there? After all, it's one of the biggest houses in the village. She might look on it as some kind of squire's house. If he's so much money why do they live in a suburban box, even if it is a lot bigger than most boxes!'

They tossed around a few more ideas, but came to no conclusions. Melanie went home, her mind in a whirl. The only thing she could do was wait, and ask Paul outright next time he came.

The next few weeks were increasingly fraught. Almost every day, it seemed, Melanie discovered a shrub uprooted, flowers in their prime chopped down, areas where it seemed a tub of weedkiller had been tipped, and the occasional branch of a larger tree broken off. As well as her normal work she was kept busy driving round to garden centres in her old car to find replacements, where she did not have spare shrubs herself, or they were too small to fit into the display.

The damage was always done at

night. Melanie took to making the rounds at odd times during the night, and Jim kept watch at weekends, but they never caught anyone. The boundary hedges were thick, but not impassable. A determined person could get in through various routes, and it was impossible to stop them all.

'Shall I get another night-watchman?' she asked Jane one morning when she'd overslept through sheer exhaustion. 'I can't keep this up, never sleeping properly.'

'It would cost a good deal more than the cost of replacing the plants,' Jane said. 'You can't afford it, Mel. They are irritating, but only niggling bits of damage.'

'So grin and let them get on with it? I just want to catch whoever it is and fry him in oil!'

'I can't see that Mr Seton-Woodward, or her, creeping round in the dark with a pair of shears or an axe,' Jane said. 'It can't be Tom, and I really can't see anyone in the village wanting to harm you.'

'So that leaves the mysterious property developer.'

She tried to stay calm, deal with the irritations as they occurred, and concentrate on making the garden look as good as possible for the final opening week. On the day before she was checking round, she was suddenly aware of an unusual silence from the poultry cages. She'd grown used to the constant clucking whenever she was in this part of the garden.

They'd been fed first thing in the morning, and she'd collected the eggs at the same time, as usual. Normally the fowl spent the day scratching around contentedly in their enclosures. Had they got out somehow and strayed? She went quickly to the pens, which were at the far end of the garden before the orchard slope began. The doors seemed to be shut, but as she came closer she could see stray feathers caught on the wires, and heaps of feathered corpses in each pen. She went inside the first one, and kneeled down beside the bantams. Their bodies were still warm, but this wasn't the work of a fox. Their necks had been wrung.

It was such wanton cruelty! Melanie struggled to keep back the tears, but they flowed down her cheeks. She'd rather they attacked her than these helpless creatures! She barely heard the voice behind her, but when her name was repeated, she turned round and saw Paul, an appalled expression on his face, looking down at the carnage.

'Mel, sweetheart, when did this happen?' he asked, and kneeled down beside her to pull her into his arms.

She sniffed, and buried her face in his sweater. His arms round her were so comforting.

'I've just found them. They're still warm, and they were OK an hour ago. Oh, if I can find out who did this I'll wring their neck! It's bad enough when they damage the shrubs, but to kill hens! Just to get at me for some reason! It's barbarous!'

He pulled her to her feet.

'We'll send for the police.'

'What can they do? They haven't been able to find out who's responsible, and after a while it gets tedious ringing up to complain yet another plant's been ripped out. They don't think it's serious, and compared with the other crimes they're faced with, it's trivial! But it matters to me!'

Melanie realised she was standing close to him, and his arms were round her, holding her tight. She wanted to lay her head on his shoulders and weep, but that would get her nowhere. She pulled away, but let him put his arm round her as he led her to a nearby bench.

'More has been happening? Tell me,' he said gently.

'Where can I start? It's been almost every day, little things, for the past two months.'

She told him about some of the damage, and her suspicions that it was someone wanting to buy her out.

'Why did you ask to be told if the Court came on the market?' she asked him.

'How did you know I had?'

'Never mind that. Why, Paul? What does it mean to you? What do you do for a living?'

He shook his head. 'Melanie, you'll have to trust me for a while longer. I can't tell you that, not yet, but I've no ulterior designs on the Court, I promise. Now go in and tidy up. I'll contact the police, and I think we'd better ask Jason to come back.'

10

Melanie looked up at him, frowning. He looked sincere, but why couldn't he tell her what his job was? How could it be so secret, if it were not connected with the desire of someone to buy her home?

'I don't want to accept favours from you, Paul, not if you can't trust me and answer reasonable questions. I'm grateful for all you've done, but how do I know it's not for your benefit, rather than mine? No, I won't have Jason. If the entire garden is ruined, so be it!'

'You're being childish!'

She stiffened. 'If that's what you think, there's no more to be said. Susie will show you your room. It's the same one.'

Ignoring his attempts to call her back she almost ran through the garden towards the house. Fortunately Jane wasn't in the kitchen, and she was able to get to her room and wash the tear stains from her face without being seen. She spent the rest of the day baking cakes for the visitors, sure that Paul would not attempt to talk to her when there were constant comings and goings through the kitchen. Susie, looking at her rather oddly, informed her he had left as soon as he'd put his case in his room, and said he wouldn't be back until late that night.

He hadn't returned by the time she went to bed, and she slept only fitfully until a sudden roar of an engine close beneath her window brought her fully awake.

'What? How on earth?'

She staggered out of bed, groping towards the window. It was a moonless night, but there were lights swerving round the garden dipping and swaying crazily like searchlights. It was a moment before she realised that at least three motorbikes were being ridden round and round the garden, ploughing up the grass and crashing through the shrubberies and flower beds. Appalled, she could see the destruction in the glare of their headlamps, as they circled and wrecked her precious plants.

Grabbing her dressing-gown, she dragged it on as she ran down the stairs. Forgetting her anger with Paul, she hammered on his door but there was no reply. Was he still out? She had no idea of the time, but thought it was well after midnight. By the time she got downstairs and out into the garden, all she could see were the red tail lamps as the bikers rode off down the drive. Her shoulders sagged. There'd be no chance of catching them now.

She took a torch, thrust her bare feet into the boots by the back door, and went out to see how much damage had been done. Deep ruts and skid marks scarred the lawns, where they seemed to have done racing turns. The flower borders were ruined where the wheels had crushed the plants, tearing some of them up and scattering debris in the path of the bikes. Shrubs were broken, branches littering the ground.

Melanie took several deep breaths. Her garden was wrecked. There wasn't an earthly chance of restoring it before the opening later that day. More than regretting losing her chance of the prize she felt a deep fury towards anyone who had caused this wanton desecration.

There was nothing to be done. For a brief moment she wondered if it was all worthwhile. She would not go back to London, but she could sell up, give up the struggle, and find a job anywhere, in some anonymous town, and live a peaceful life without all this aggravation. Then she drew back her shoulders. She was not going to give up! She'd show them, whoever they were, and she'd make a success of her garden and her guest house.

The sky was just beginning to lighten. She had thought it was earlier, but soon it would be light enough to see, to start work repairing the worst of the damage. She put on the kettle and while it boiled ran upstairs to drag on jeans and a sweater. A cup of tea, and then she could at least sweep the debris away from the paths. Perhaps, in daylight, it wouldn't look so bad.

She was drinking coffee and nibbling at a slice of toast she didn't really want when Paul walked into the kitchen.

'Mel, what are you doing up so late?'

'Late? It's early,' she said, glancing at the clock on the wall, wondering where he had been until five in the morning.

'I had a sudden call, an emergency, and had to go back to London, but I decided to drive back during the night rather than go to my flat. Can I have a coffee, please?'

Melanie stood up.

'Help yourself, there's more in the machine. I have work to do.'

'Melanie, don't be like this with me! I can explain in a few days.'

'Sure. But I still have work to do.'

She went outside, taking the key to the tool shed. Her mind was whirling.

Could Paul have been one of the bikers? He'd had plenty of time to stash a bike somewhere, change into normal clothes, and drive back here. She didn't want to believe that, but a sudden trip to London, some emergency which had occupied half the night, seemed rather far-fetched.

She rounded the corner and stopped suddenly. The tool shed door had been wrenched off its hinges, and was hanging from the stout padlock she had been using every since the first attack on her property. Her tools were in a mess, scattered around and soon she saw the wooden handles of the spades and forks, the rakes and hoes and brooms, had been broken. She saw the batteries of both the ride-on and the hand mower tossed into a corner, their acid dripping out, and the hover mower and strimmer handles had been wrenched and twisted so as to make them unusable. Canes had been broken and tossed aside.

The greenhouses! She turned and

ran, and her worst fears were realised. Glass had been carefully removed from the frame, the panes laid in a neat pile, and sacking placed over them to smother the sound of them being smashed. The plants inside, the carefully-tended seed trays and pots, where she was growing the plants for next year, had all been swept to the floor. Sacks of compost and bark and fertiliser had been ripped open and tipped on to the general mess.

It had been a carefully-planned operation. To do all this so systematically would have taken at least an hour, even with three or four men, and this had been done before the final flourish, the manic bike ride.

In one night, a few hours, they had caused thousands of pounds worth of damage, and destroyed months of careful work and planning. Melanie's resolution almost failed her. She sank on to an upturned bucket and put her head in her hands. How on earth was she going to recover from this disaster?

The sound of crunching glass made her look up.

'What do you want now?' she demanded, rising to confront Paul.

He was looking round, lips compressed. She had never seen him so grim-faced.

'To see your handiwork?' she ground out in fury.

'Mel! Surely you can't imagine I did this.'

'I have no idea who did it! But you weren't here, you were off on some mysterious trip to London and you won't tell me what you do. You're interested in the possible sale of the Court, there's a property developer trying to buy it, and why shouldn't that be you?'

'I've said I'll explain. There are reasons I can't tell you about my job, or my interest in the Court, but not until this week is over! Is there any chance of getting some of this damage put right quickly?'

'Why should you care? No, there

isn't. Please can I get past? I'm going to phone the police.'

He let her go, and she walked swiftly to the house, planning what she should say, struggling to calm herself, or they'd think she was hysterical. She'd almost reached the kitchen door when she heard the sound of a car on the drive. Now what? Who was coming so early? It was still too early for Jane and Susie.

She went round the house and saw a tall, thin young man easing himself out of a small car. He turned and saw her, smiled, and walked towards her, holding out his hand.

'Good morning. Miss Hetherington? I'm Chris Towers, reporter on the Westbridge Chronicle. I understand you've been the target of various sabotage attacks on your garden.' He glanced round, and his eyes grew wider. 'Wow? Is this another?'

'Yes, it is!' Melanie snapped. 'How is it you come out here at the crack of dawn, just after this latest outrage?'

'I had a phone call. Someone rang to

say there's been a big upset. I thought it was you.'

Melanie glared at him. 'No, it was not me! Was it a woman?'

'Actually, I couldn't tell. It was a deep voice, could have been a man, come to think of it. Is this what they've done? Can I take some pictures? I understand you were in the running for the Jubilee prize for these open garden weeks?' he went on, taking a small camera from his pocket and starting to snap away without waiting for her permission.

Melanie felt too weary to protest.

'I suppose if people see what's been done, it might help to catch the vandals who did it,' she said.

'They say it's rivals for the prize,' Chris Towers went on, still snapping away as he moved towards the rear of the house. 'Lord, this is even worse! How did they cause such a mess?'

'Motorbikes, at least three. I was woken by the row.'

'You must be devastated. What were

your feelings when you realised what was happening?'

'What do you expect? Mr Towers, take what photos you like, but I don't think it was my rivals who did it. I believe it's someone who wants to scare me away, buy me out in order to make a vast profit building houses here. Now do excuse me. I was on the point of telephoning the police.'

Several times that day Paul tried to speak to Melanie, but she remained distant. In the end he gave up and went out late in the afternoon. She was busy dealing with the police, her insurance company, Angela and numerous friends. There was no point in starting to clear up, or in opening. Susie painted a large notice to put outside the gates — **Garden closed due to vandalism**, and they kept the gates locked. Jim pottered around, ready to open to the official visitors, and Jane spent part of the morning putting Melanie's cakes in the freezer.

'They'll do for next time, or for the

guests,' she said.

Paul had not returned by the time Melanie, exhausted, crawled into bed. She didn't want to think about him, but despite her exhaustion her mind churned round with speculations. He'd been so supportive before. She'd grown to like him more than she'd admitted to herself. It had seemed, in June, that he was working towards more than just a casual friendship, and Melanie had allowed herself to dream that here, at last, was a man she could spend her life with. Now it was all ruined. His secrecy, the suspicions she still harboured, which had become stronger the past few week, came between them. There was no possibility he could explain these away.

Heavy-eyed, she lay in bed until she heard Jane's car drive up. There was nothing to be done in the garden, no point or urgency in trying to make it look decent. She'd do it gradually, during the winter, in between catering for her groups of students on the various courses she'd arranged. She went downstairs to find Jane and Susie poring over one of the tabloid newspapers.

'Mel, look at this! We're famous!' Susie said.

She thrust the paper, open at a double-page spread, with several pictures of her ruined garden, including one of the greenhouse. **Guest House Garden Target for Vandals**, in huge letters, screamed across both pages. Horrified, she read the text.

Westford Court, upmarket guest house with famous gardens, has been hit many times during the year since the former proprietor, Mr Gerald Hetherington, died. His daughter, Melanie, a florist, who is taking a break from her previous job with a prestigious West End firm, is at present running the guest house. She believes the damage to be caused either by a rival for the Westford Garden Jubilee Prize, or a property developer who wants to drive her away and buy the property at a low price.

It went on, quoting several of the villagers, whose opinions ranged between Tom's genuine sorrow at the mindless wrecking of a beautiful garden, to the comment that she could see no merit in a hodge-podge of styles from Mrs Seton-Woodward.

What will be the next thing to hit florist, Melanie, who is starting a new venture, running a variety of residential courses during the winter months? If it is a garden rival, will they be content to have spoiled her chances? If it is a developer, what tricks will he get up to next? So far only the garden has been attacked, but will the house be next?

Melanie groaned. 'This is all we need! National coverage! I want to kill that Chris Towers!'

'It must be him, making a bit on the side,' Jane said. 'I've heard that's what they do. He couldn't wait for next week's Chronicle to come out.'

'No doubt the rest of the Press pack will be down on us today. Susie, if they phone, say it's in the hands of the police, otherwise no comment. If they come in person, don't let them in. We'd better give all the guests keys. We can't risk leaving the front door unlocked.'

Susie nodded and went to see to it. Melanie tried to concentrate on paper work in her office, fielding telephone calls when Susie was doing other jobs. By lunchtime she was becoming seriously worried. Ten students had rung to withdraw from the pre-Christmas courses. If twice that number followed suit, she would be in danger of not even clearing her expenses, let alone making any profit. Some had manufactured excuses of other commitments, a couple of women said their husbands didn't think it was a good idea for them to stay at a place where such worrying things happened, and one said outright she had no intention of getting caught up in a silly feud which looked like getting out of hand and dangerous.

'Ought I to cancel them all?' she asked Jane while they were sitting down to a salad lunch. 'If I go ahead with only half the number of students, I'll make a loss.'

'You're not usually so defeatist,' Jane rallied her. 'It's free publicity for the courses, and I'll bet there will be some people who want to come just because they get a thrill from the thought of danger.'

Jane was proved right when three people rang that afternoon to ask for details of the courses, and if there were still vacancies. They might be sensation-seekers, but their money was as good as anyone else's, and Melanie was partially reassured. She still had the deposits the others had paid, which were non-returnable. It wasn't as dire as she'd first thought.

A couple of the tutors rang, and at first Melanie suspected they meant to cry off, but they were supportive, encouraging her in her determination not to give in, not to succumb to vague threats.

'Stick it out, lass,' one of the local

painters advised. 'If it is one of the garden crowd, it'll be over by now. Shame about the prize, but everyone in the village knows you'd have won it in normal circumstances.'

11

'I'm glad you won, Tom,' Melanie said a week later, in the village hall on the Sunday evening after the gardens finally closed.

The prizes had been announced. Because of what had happened at the Court there were more journalists there than had been expected, and the sum raised for the hospice was almost twice their previous best.

'You'll be having people from that magazine round soon, the one that's featuring the winning garden. Or have they already been in touch?' she went on.

'Not yet,' Tom replied.

'What beats me,' Mrs Travers said, 'is how they can show pictures of the gardens at all the seasons. After all, it's a whole year of competition.'

'Oh, they had a photographer here, I

expect. Lots of people were taking photos. I hope they include some of the other gardens. Yours, for instance, Melanie. It should have been you winning,' Tom said. 'It would have been if you hadn't had all that damage done. Even with what happened the first two opening weeks, you were ahead of me.'

'Well, never mind. It can't make any difference to Dad, and in fact it's given me the opportunity for some changes. I'd never have been able to destroy what Dad had created, but those bikers did that.'

'What ideas?' Tom asked. 'How are you going to change it?'

Melanie paused. 'I'll extend the vegetable garden, and get more poultry. I know that makes more work, but I shall cut down on the flower beds to compensate. Fresh eggs and vegetables are always appreciated.'

'You're right there. Will you just grass over the beds?'

'Probably, for the moment, but I've bigger plans for when I can afford it.

I've been thinking how I can attract more families to come. I'm going to put in a covered swimming pool and a tennis court.'

'Have you costed this?' Tom asked, looking worried.

Melanie smiled at him.

'There has been some insurance money, but these are just vague plans for the future, when I can afford it.'

'Why don't you get young Daniel Forster to give you advice? He's an architect, after all. I saw him around earlier. Yes, there he is, talking to that nice Mr Hunt. I'll go and fetch him.'

Melanie opened her mouth to protest, but Tom was gone. He was anxious to be helpful, knowing how disappointed she was, but she didn't want to get involved with Michael's brother. It could be embarrassing. However, Daniel came back with Tom, smiling broadly.

'I hear you want my almost-professional advice,' he said, grinning.

He was too like Michael for comfort.

Melanie, urged on by Tom, explained her ideas.

'Can I come round soon and have a look? It's ages since I was at the Court. Heard you've been having a lot of trouble.'

'You could say that.'

'Tomorrow afternoon then?'

She could not avoid it, so Melanie nodded.

'See you, then. Thanks.'

Daniel nodded and moved away, and Melanie saw Paul approaching. Paul was still at the Court, but during the past week she had avoided him as much as possible, and didn't know whether to be glad or sorry that he would be departing on Tuesday. If he were not involved with her problems, not a property developer, she'd wronged him, and he'd never forgive her. If he were, he might try to persuade her to sell.

She tried to escape through the kitchen, but Mrs Travers detained her, clutching at her arm, and the opportunity was gone.

'Can I give you a lift home, Mel?' Paul asked. 'I hear your car's got problems.'

'I came on my bike. Thanks, but there's no need.'

'It's dark, and wet and windy. Leave your bike here and collect it tomorrow.'

'No, thank you. I need it first thing in the morning.'

'As you wish,' he said, sighing and turning away.

By the time Melanie was riding up the drive of the Court she was wondering if she had been stupid. She was soaked, exhausted and had had to dive into the shelter of the hedges three times when cars had swept by too close, drenching her with muddy spray. To her relief, Paul was not around, though his car was parked near the front door, and she was able to get to her room unobserved.

She was in her office the following morning when Daniel arrived. She had her own sketches of what she wanted spread out over the desk, and swept them into a pile when Susie asked her over the intercom if she was ready. Then he knocked briefly and came in. Behind him was Michael, who closed the door firmly behind him.

'I wasn't expecting you,' she said in surprise. 'I don't think you can advise me on building plans.'

He smiled, crossed the room, and before she could evade him, kissed her on the cheek.

'Melanie, how good to see you again. Daniel tells me you are going to struggle on, with even more ambitious plans, when I have the perfect solution for us to make pots of lovely lolly.'

'I told you, it's not what I want. I hope we are not going to waste time in pointless argument.'

'Not pointless, my dear. Look, I'll be frank with you. I can see a great opportunity here at the Court. I'm offering you the chance of coming in with me, but if you don't then I'll force you out, and reap the profits myself.'

Melanie stared at him, realisation

gradually dawning.

'It's been you all the time! You've been causing the damage!'

She was thinking back to the first occasion, when he'd been in the area, staying with Angela or actually in this house.

'But you couldn't have been here practically every night the past couple of months!'

Michael glanced across at Daniel, a complacent smile on his lips.

'I couldn't,' he agreed.

Melanie saw that Daniel was grinning, too. It had been him, and no doubt some of his biker friends, who had created such mayhem. She reached for the phone on her desk, but Michael grabbed it from her.

'No, you don't. It's your word against both of us. No-one can prove anything.'

'Why?' Melanie demanded.

'Money, my sweet. This place is worth a fortune if we can get planning permission for more houses. Are you going to be sensible, and come in with us while you can, or do we have to force your hand?'

'You mean cause more damage? No, Michael, I'll never sell to you, whatever you threaten!'

'You will, Melanie. In fact I have the documents here, a contract to sell me the house. If you won't sign it now you'll come away with us somewhere very uncomfortable until you are begging to be allowed to sign.'

'Go to blazes! Even if I did sign you'd have to let me go, and no contract signed under duress would be valid!'

'But we wouldn't let you go until after completion, my dear. We have solicitors all ready to do the work. Grab her, Dan!'

Melanie struggled, but they were both strong men, and they swiftly thrust a gag into her mouth and pushed her towards the outer door.

'The van's just outside. You won't be seen, and we'll send a message to explain a sudden emergency came up, so no-one will worry,' Michael said, and then gave an odd sort of gurgle and collapsed to the ground.

Daniel swung round in alarm, and received a well-aimed punch on the jaw. He collapsed on top of his brother.

'Susie! Do you have that parcel tape?'

Melanie was tearing the gag out of her mouth.

'Paul!' she gasped as she spat out the fabric. 'How did you know?'

He grinned up at her, busy winding yards of strong parcel tape round Michael's arms to tie them together. He bound his ankles, too, and then turned his attention to Daniel and tied him up as well. The brothers were beginning to come to, groaning and swearing.

'Best tape their mouths, too. They're not going to be very pleased. Can I ring the police now?' Susie asked, her voice shrill with excitement.

'Yes. And then ask your mother to bring a pot of tea. We need one.'

Susie vanished, and Melanie, her

mind buzzing with questions, sat down by the desk.

'How did you know? Oh, I suppose I should thank you. I do.' She shuddered. 'How could they imagine they'd get away with it?'

'I think your Michael was hoping to get you on your own and try a spot of persuasion. You might have gone along with him when he'd had time to tell you of the millions he was doubtless hoping to make.'

'He's not my Michael! And I'd never have agreed! But how did you know what was happening?'

'You left the intercom switched on, and Susie and I heard it all. I was just going through the hall when she waved to me to stop and listen.'

'Thank goodness she did! Paul, I'm so sorry. I was even suspecting you at times!'

'Because I wouldn't tell you what my job is?'

Melanie nodded. 'I didn't know what to believe, and you were so mysterious, even when I asked outright.'

Jane came in then, agog to hear what had happened, and before it had been explained, the police arrived. It was an hour later before they had gone, taking the Forster brothers with them and promising they'd get heavy sentences for both the damage they'd caused and their attempted abduction.

'Now, can you tell me?' Melanie asked Paul when Jane firmly ushered Susie, still excited, out of the office.

He leaned across and made sure the intercom was off.

'My real name's Jean-Paul Hunter,' he admitted.

Melanie's eyes widened. 'The photographer? You take all those wonderful wildlife photographs? They are always in the supplements and the glossy magazines. But why the secrecy? Why use a different name?'

'I was here to take photos of the gardens, for that article. But the idea was that I took them like an ordinary tourist, nothing posed, except at the end, for the winner. I couldn't let anyone know what I was doing, as it could have caused all sorts of complications if people knew why I was here.'

'I suppose so.'

'I have a very complete record of your garden before any of the damage was inflicted,' he said. 'When I told the editor what was happening he said he wanted a feature on your garden, too, before the damage and how you managed to restore it. I suppose we'll have to wait until after the trial now, as my photos might be needed as evidence. Tell me, was it really all over between you and Michael?'

'Yes, it certainly was, months ago.'

'Then you could be looking for another partner for the business?'

'I have a mortgage, and I don't think I could work with anyone else.'

'Not even me?'

'You? But why? You have your own career.'

'But I don't have a home, or a wife, and I feel the lack of both. Melanie, I wanted you when I first met you, but I was wary. It was too soon after Elizabeth. Then I came to realise how dedicated you are. Sweetheart, I'm trying to say, in a rather gauche manner, that I've fallen in love with you. I want to marry you. Have I any chance at all?'

Melanie was breathing rather hard.

'I — Paul, I never thought I had a chance with you, and it's being so uncertain that's made me so evil-tempered this past week. I couldn't bear the thought you might be trying to get the Court, to develop it.'

'But I am,' he said, and laughed. 'Melanie, my love, I heard all about your plans from Mrs Travers, and with the money I can put in, you can go ahead with them as soon as you like.'

Melanie gulped, and he caught her to him. It was the most satisfying of kisses. When she came up for air she grinned at him.

'Those unexplained visits to Mrs Travers and Mrs Seton-Woodward?'

'Getting to know the people I'd been tipped might stand a chance of the prize. Melanie, darling, I'm so sorry I wasn't able to protect your garden so that you could win it.'

'Never mind,' she whispered, as she went back into his arms, 'I'm getting a far better prize. I'm getting you.'

THE END

We do hope that you have enjoyed reading this large print book.

Did you know that all of our titles are available for purchase?

We publish a wide range of high quality large print books including:
Romances, Mysteries, Classics
General Fiction
Non Fiction and Westerns

Special interest titles available in large print are:
The Little Oxford Dictionary
Music Book, Song Book
Hymn Book, Service Book

Also available from us courtesy of Oxford University Press:
Young Readers' Dictionary
(large print edition)
Young Readers' Thesaurus
(large print edition)

For further information or a free brochure, please contact us at:
Ulverscroft Large Print Books Ltd.,
The Green, Bradgate Road, Anstey,
Leicester, LE7 7FU, England.
Tel: (00 44) **0116 236 4325**
Fax: (00 44) **0116 234 0205**

Other titles in the
Linford Romance Library:

A HEART DIVIDED

Karen Abbott

During World War Two, the German occupation of Ile D'Oleron, off the west coast of France, brings fear and hardship to the islanders. As the underground freedom-fighters strive to liberate their beloved island, Florentine Devreux finds her heart torn between two brothers. But it seems she has fallen in love with the wrong one! The events following the Normandy landings force her to think again — but has her change of heart come too late?

SHADOW OF THE FLAME

Sheila Belshaw

When zoology student Lisa Ryding first meets wildlife film-maker Guy Barrington at Oxford University, she is prepared to follow him to the ends of the earth. But a secret too tragic for Guy to reveal makes this impossible. Five years later, they are thrown together on a remote game reserve in Zambia by their mutual passion to save the elephant from extinction. When Guy is bitten by a snake and nearly dies, Lisa realises that nothing will ever change her love for him and her only salvation will be to never see him again.